SOULS OF SCAPA FLOW

SOULS OF SCAPA FLOW

S.D. Read

The Book Guild

First published in Great Britain in 2025 by
The Book Guild Ltd
Unit E2 Airfield Business Park,
Harrison Road, Market Harborough,
Leicestershire. LE16 7UL
Tel: 0116 2792299
www.bookguild.co.uk
Email: info@bookguild.co.uk

The manufacturer's authorised representative in the EU
for product safety is Authorised Rep Compliance Ltd,
71 Lower Baggot Street, Dublin D02 P593 Ireland (www.arccompliance.com)

The SS Reginald was deliberately sunk during WWI as a blockship, to prevent U
Boats from entering Scapa Flow, and is still visible (as pictured on the cover).

Typeset in 11pt Minion Pro

Printed and bound in Great Britain by 4edge Limited

ISBN 978 1835743 294

British Library Cataloguing in Publication Data.
A catalogue record for this book is available from the British Library.

For Carolyn

PROLOGUE

9th July 1917

Alex MacKay should have been asleep in bed. It was nearly twenty past eleven at night, yet he was sat cross-legged in rough grass, sweeping binoculars greedily over an array of warships at rest in the Orkney twilight. He had a practised routine of artfully placing two pillows lengthways in his bed, climbing out the window, shinning down the drainpipe, then sprinting low to his vantage point like a soldier under fire to avoid being seen. His evening perch afforded an elevated view beyond Hoy's shores, out over the island of Flotta and the waters of Scapa Flow, to the dark, low folds of Orkney's mainland beyond.

Scapa Flow, two Norse words the war had made common parlance across the British Empire and beyond. Its deep waters, largely enveloped by the islands of

Orkney, offered a protected anchorage from which the Royal Navy could control the North Sea. At twelve years old, Alex didn't really care about why the Navy was there, only that it was. He devoured the newspapers for any news of the fleet, though didn't need a broadsheet to tell him there were nearly two hundred ships in front of him that evening.

Alex settled his magnified gaze on a battleship anchored close to Flotta and smiled to himself at the sight. *HMS Vanguard* was a ship he knew well. He'd seen it many times and could recite the details he'd written about it in his scrapbook:

St Vincent Class Dreadnought
Length: 536 feet
19,700 tons
5 pairs of 12-inch guns
14×4-inch guns
2×3-inch anti-aircraft guns
13×18-inch torpedo tubes
13×4-inch anti-torpedo guns
Top speed: 24 knots

Alex had seen it return to the anchorage earlier that evening, presumably after an exercise, and though the light was fading, he could clearly discern the movement of sailors on its decks like busy ants, scurrying beneath the massive guns.

As he focused on the front turret, the great ship seemed to shiver for a moment, then a tongue of angry flame leapt skywards from behind the forecastle, quickly followed by an orange fireball and a thunderous boom that made Alex flinch and drop his binoculars, before a second explosion obscured the great ship in a burgeoning cloud of fire, smoke and debris. When he tried to refocus with trembling hands, *HMS Vanguard* was gone. A slew of floating wreckage amid a slick of oil was the only trace of her and of over eight hundred men.

Alex sat for a while, mouth agape, breathing and blinking rapidly as a collective wail of alarms rang from the surrounding ships as they moved to action stations. It was if the fleet was crying for her dead.

He ran home, almost jumping tear-streaked into his mother's arms at the front door. There was no inquest into why he was outside past bedtime or a chastening slipper from his father as there had been when he was last caught. Nothing was said. It simply wasn't important tonight.

Later, as Alex lay in bed, the incredible sight of the *Vanguard*'s last moments replayed in his mind over and again. It was several hours before he succumbed to a fitful sleep. As the days passed, the shock faded and Alex gradually thought less of what he had seen that July night, but he would never forget it, especially as there was never a definitive explanation for the sinking. The resulting inquiry concluded that unstable cordite had caused *HMS Vanguard* to explode at anchor, the images of which remained in Alex's mind. They were always there, like a series of disturbing photographs in an inside pocket, which, once inadvertently touched, had to be looked at again.

Alex MacKay would live a long life tending his beef herd on Hoy, only leaving for his wartime service in the army. He saw the scuttling of the German fleet in Scapa Flow in 1919, survived the bullets and shells of Normandy in 1944 and became old enough to receive a birthday card from the Queen in 2005. Yet whenever he was asked about the wars by his family, "*HMS Vanguard*" were usually the first words he uttered. And sometimes, when those images flooded his mind once more, his eyes would brim with tears, just as they did on that hillside on Hoy in July 1917.

I

It began because of the seductive power of money. The lure of a fat, pristine wad of five thousand pounds had dissolved Callum Craigie's principles and set him on a frightening course he could never have imagined. At this moment though, as he steered the *Peedie Star* through calm waters under an open sky, life felt good. He smiled to himself at the idea of a week in Ibiza and some new alloys that he thought would take his VW Golf to a different level.

HMS Vanguard's marker buoy wasn't difficult to find, bobbing gently just to the North of Flotta, its black and yellow top easily discernible in such fine September weather. Callum turned in the open cab and shouted over his shoulder to the two Americans sat facing each other on the bench seats at the stern, already in their dry suits and prepared to dive.

'About five minutes!'

They both nodded; Dwight O'Neil also gave a thumbs-up and a Hollywood grin, while Remi Binks immediately went back to checking his kit. They sat opposite one another, which summed up so much about them. Dwight was a big, blond, bluff New Yorker, flush with money from trading on Wall Street, and Remi was a slight, dark-haired and serious ICT Manager from Boston who had to squirrel money away for his diving holidays. While Dwight was single and loudly declared his hobbies as wine, women and diving, Remi was contentedly married to Kim and spent most of his leisure time with her and their baby daughter Holly. Remi also liked baseball and followed the Red Sox on TV, while Dwight was a former Princeton Tigers quarterback and had a season ticket for the Jets.

However, they had two things in common; both were thirty-three and both loved diving. They'd met in 2022 on a dive boat taking them to Iron Bottom Sound, where the wrecks of the Battle of Guadalcanal littered the ocean floor. It had been Dwight's first trip since qualifying and he appreciated the calm reassurance of an old hand like Remi, who had been PADI-qualified since he was a teenager. They stayed in touch and 2023 saw them dive to the famed Thistlegorm in the Red Sea, after which Remi had piqued Dwight's interest when he talked about the wrecks of Scapa Flow where the Germans had scuttled their fleet in 1919.

The pair had been in Orkney almost a week, enjoying the diving to the British blockships and the German warships, Dresden, Cöln and Karlsruhe. Yet in the evenings at The Murray Arms where they stayed, Dwight had repeatedly talked about *HMS Vanguard*, the British dreadnought that mysteriously exploded in 1917. As they sat at a corner table in the cosy old bar, Remi reminded him it was a protected site.

'Come on, Remi, salvage divers have been to it time and again until the '80s. Heck, the British Navy dived on it in 2017!' implored Dwight.

'Yeah, to survey it and put a new Ensign on the hull as a memorial. It's a grave site, Dwight. Forget it.'

Earlier that day, Dwight had asked the skipper of their boat from Scapa Adventures to name his price for a dive to the *Vanguard* and the glare he'd received in response had led Dwight to think the guy was going to hit him. Undaunted, he had rung every other wreck-diving company in Orkney to ask the same question, and received the same swift, blunt rejection from them all. One guy had even shouted at him. His accent meant Dwight couldn't fully decipher the words, but the message was clear enough.

'Orkneyian dumbfucks!' spat Dwight when recalling the conversation in the bar later.

'Orcadians.'

'What?'

'The locals are called Orcadians,' replied Remi evenly, 'and keep your voice lower.'

'Whatever! They're still dumbfucks!'

'Come on, Dwight. There's no need for the prejudice and the language.'

'Gimme a break, man. You get called a jerk every second block in New York.'

'Maybe that's just you,' said Remi with a grin and Dwight laughed aloud.

'Dwight, the site's a war grave. Diving to it's illegal. No one's gonna agree to take us, and I don't know if I wanna go anyway.'

Yet, a day later, Dwight and Remi were putting their fins on and preparing to step off the *Peedie Star*, a small blue fishing boat with a white open cabin, wallowing close to the buoy that marked the resting place of *HMS Vanguard*. Pure chance had brought all three men to this point. Callum was a dive boat crewman for Scapa Adventures, lived in St Margaret's Hope and frequented The Murray Arms, where Dwight and Remi were staying. Dwight recognised the short, stocky frame and cropped ginger hair when he entered the bar and bought him a drink. An hour and two further bottles of Skull Splitter later, Callum had agreed to take them to *HMS Vanguard* for a fat fee if he could get a friend to lend him his boat.

Yet Callum wasn't so affected by his rapid consumption of Orkney's strongest brew that he didn't set some clear stipulations. He would drop them near the marker buoy, then move away under the pretence of fishing nearby and return after forty-five minutes at 6pm. The buoy was in clear sight of Flotta's oil terminal, after all, and he didn't want to be answering any difficult questions later. So, Callum insisted that it would be one short dive only, with no use of a dive marker that would show their position. *HMS Vanguard*'s buoy was to be their point of reference for being picked up instead.

As he'd swirled a single malt round his tumbler, Remi had remained dubious about the risks and the rightness of what Dwight had planned, while his companion clapped

Callum on the back as they propped up the bar, saying, 'Hell, yeah! We're in your hands, man!'

Now they were indeed in Callum's hands, dependent on him finding them after the dive amid strong currents, though visibility was good and the water mercifully calm, with only a slight swell. As Remi stood at the boat's stern and looked at the wreck buoy with its bright yellow panel declaring "VANGUARD WRECK" in simple black letters, he felt uncharacteristically sick. He was an excellent diver, calm and economical with his breathing, but at this moment he was everything he didn't expect or want to be – anxious and conflicted about visiting a war grave.

Dwight broke his chain of thought. 'OK, bro. Let's rock 'n' roll.'

Remi nodded, climbed on to the seat and stepped over the side. Once in the water, they fitted their masks and respirators, started their smartphone-like dive computers simultaneously and, with a joint thumbs-down, opened their buoyancy control vests and began their descent in a swirl of bubbles. It grew darker as they dropped deeper into this thrilling, different world. Remi was now focused on the dive.

The plan was to stop first at fifty feet, where they should be level with the highest parts of the ship. Once they found the bow, they would descend another fifty-five feet to just above the seabed and swim south from one end of the wreck site to the other.

As they levelled off, they gave each other the OK sign to indicate there were no problems as a large pollock moved lazily in and out of view in the translucent green gloom.

Dwight's diving torch clicked on and Remi followed suit. The sharp shafts of brightness reflected across a shoal of flitting silver bellies as the two beams crossed, probing the water ahead like ghostly searchlights. Almost immediately, the torches played over a sharp metallic shape and Remi felt a surge of adrenaline. Less than forty feet away, the bow of *HMS Vanguard* pointed upwards. It was as if the great ship was emerging from the seabed.

Dwight made straight towards it, his light illuminating the rivetted, rusted plates encrusted with marine life. Remi was close behind, his eyes wide behind his mask. To him, shipwrecks were a curious combination of enthralling history and unsettling eeriness. *HMS Vanguard* proved to be no exception. As they came within touching distance, they were dwarfed by the detached front bow standing as high as a house. It was like a piece from some terrible jigsaw, leaving Remi transfixed but also profoundly sad.

Dwight seemed excitedly animated as usual, moving beyond the broken bow into an open area of water, before giving an extravagant thumbs-down. He descended as soon as Remi reciprocated to confirm he too was ready to go deeper. It was a slow, careful manoeuvre with torch lights pointing down to avoid colliding with the wreck or hitting the seabed and throwing up a spray of blinding silt and gravel. Once they were nine feet from the bottom, they levelled out and set a southerly course with their compasses, before swimming steadily and studiously forward.

Within seconds they knew their course was correct as their lights picked out the remains of a gun turret rising drunkenly askew from the seabed like a massive, battered drum. As they moved past the neutered turret, from which the guns had long been removed as salvage, they looked down on a debris field of tangled rusting remains. Much appeared as jumbled metal, but here and there, things were recognisable; the bent foremast, a twisted deck rail, a capstan with barnacles. An encrusted brass porthole lay alone, its shattered glass glinting in the torchlight like a blinded eye. Things that were once pristine and alive with use now lay smashed and decaying.

Even though Remi had done some research, it still hadn't prepared him for how little of the middle section was discernible as a ship. He shuddered inwardly at the magnitude of the explosion that had reduced it to this and condemned all but two of those on board to such an untimely end. Suddenly, he felt like an intruder, an unwanted guest at a funeral, observing the misery of others.

Dwight, meanwhile, was revelling in the dive. *It wasn't the biggest wreck he'd seen – heck, there wasn't really a lot there – but to see what other modern divers didn't and also what they shouldn't was a definite thrill. After all, a sneaky joint behind the gym at college was always way better than one at a party.*

As he kicked languidly and scanned the scattered remnants of the ship, Dwight spotted something different: a small glimpse of white and blue among the rusting, broken brown. He dived down and shone his light close to, revealing the lip of a blue and white plate peeping out of the silt. Dwight smiled to himself and reached carefully for it, easing it upwards and trying not to disturb the seabed too much. As he freed it, he felt a sharp pain in his right index finger, like the piercing of a needle, and dropped the object in a spray of silt. He assumed he must have caught the spine of a sea urchin or a sharp remnant of mollusc, though he couldn't see anything stuck in his glove. As he was examining himself, the beam of Remi's light moved over him and his buddy came close, concern clear in his eyes. There was no pain now and nothing to see, so Dwight responded with an OK sign and looked for the object once more in the settling silt. He spotted it straight away. It seemed to sit looking at him. It was a mess plate, white, with the traditional blue floral pattern round its rim and "MESS No. 12" marked under a blue crown in its centre. Dwight reached down, more tentatively, as if it were alive somehow, but this time he simply lifted it clear of the seabed. He held it up for Remi to see and could have predicted his reaction.

Dwight placed the plate in his dive bag and Remi shook his head violently. *Damn you, Remi, you're not my dad,* thought Dwight as he shone the light back to where he'd found the plate. There was a second glint of white and blue and when he felt in the silt, he discovered a second rim close behind the first. Dwight surmised the plates had been in some sort of rack or wooden cupboard that had long since rotted away. He was practically blind in a fog of particles as he felt for the second and third plates, placing them in his bag before ascending slightly so he could escape the silt storm he'd created. After adjusting the bag so it sat on his hip, Dwight checked his dive computer, indicating they still had another eight of their fifteen minutes at 110 feet, enough time to reach the stern and cover the length of the dive site.

Remi knew he was breathing faster than he should, but he was angry. An illicit dive was one thing; taking artefacts from a war grave was something else entirely. At that moment he fought the urge to surface and tell Dwight some home truths; he knew they had to stay together for safety reasons. He too was keeping a close check on the time and the one consolation was that there wasn't long left for Dwight to do anything else stupid.

So, Remi kicked on behind Dwight as they swam above the debris until they spotted what remained of X Turret. Like A Turret, the first one they'd seen, it was a large solid cylinder disgorging entrails of metal from the top. As they moved to its left, Y Turret also came into hazy view, with the silhouette of the ship's stern rising behind it.

They closed on *Vanguard*'s stern, lying on its port side. Dwight pointed his beam downwards to illuminate the port rudder, half buried in the silt, just as a large wrasse cruised past it, glinting in the shaft of light. Remi then gestured to Dwight to follow the curve of the stern round. It grew darker as they swam in the shade of the ship, their torches offering the only real illumination, and the water became noticeably colder on their hands and feet.

On reaching the port side, Remi found what he was looking for: the word "VANGUARD" still showing in fading white letters, despite the scabbing marine life mottling the ship. Remi shook his head at the sight while Dwight was ruing the fact he'd agreed not to bring a camera. Time underwater was now short and they concluded the dive by swimming over the stern deck, where a gun fringed with rusticles stood alone and redundant.

They ascended steadily to a depth of fifteen feet over three minutes, then levelled out for another three as a precaution against "the bends". As they remained suspended in the water, the blurred outline of the wreck site just visible below, Remi was wrestling with mixed emotions. Seeing the *Vanguard* was an amazing experience, one few divers would ever have, but it just felt wrong. And as for Dwight's pilfering, Remi was struggling to find the words for what he wanted to say once they were on the boat.

When they finally surfaced, they were a hundred yards or so from the memorial buoy, as expected. Remi pointed towards it and they swam face down to gain maximum power from their fins, pausing occasionally to check their course. As they raised their heads close to the buoy, they heard, then saw, the blue hull and white wheelhouse of the *Peedie Star*, puttering towards them. Within minutes, with Callum's help and the aid of a ladder, they were on board, sitting opposite each other. Remi fixed Dwight with a glare.

'What's eating you, man?' asked Dwight.

'You know what, Dwight!'

'A few freakin' plates! What's the big deal?' said Dwight, as he brought them out of his dive bag. He held one up with a defiant smile. Remi's face didn't change. Callum, who had turned to see what the raised voices were for, frowned too at the sight of the mess plate.

Callum turned back to the wheel with a slight shake of his head, keen to move away from the *Vanguard*'s buoy as soon as possible, but as he placed his hand on the shift lever the boat cut out. He reached for the ignition, then suddenly lurched sideways and staggered as a big wave slapped into them and the *Peedie Star* began to roll violently.

Callum held on to the frame of the wheelhouse as he turned to look at the sky. The few high clouds moved slowly yet the wind was suddenly whipping the waves into a frenzy, but when he spotted a trawler a quarter of a mile away, there was no pitch or roll. He was an experienced sailor and knew the Flow as well as most, but this was like some strange micro-climate.

Dwight and Remi had stopped changing and were holding on to the bench seats as they rose and fell opposite each other as if on a see-saw. Remi looked fearful; Dwight raised a quizzical eyebrow at Callum. At a loss, Callum turned back into the wheelhouse where, thankfully, the engine coughed then fired, and they started to move, corkscrewing forwards with water spilling over the gunwales. Within a minute, the wind died down and the sea calmed once again.

Remi looked back towards the *Vanguard*'s buoy. It was swaying like a pendulum on a foaming whirlpool, yet the rest of the water was calm. Even Dwight looked unnerved. They all exchanged glances, but no one spoke until they stepped ashore half an hour later.

2

Dwight and Remi sat opposite each other, either side of a small table in The Murray Arms restaurant, waiting for their dessert. Their heads were close as they simultaneously reached for their beer glasses, yet they were poles apart on the issue of the mess plates. Dwight had cleaned them on their return and they were pristine, save some slight yellowing on the rim of one, presumably the first that he'd seen poking out of the silt.

'Great dive today, buddy, huh?' said Dwight.

He was met by pursed lips and a flinty stare from Remi, who'd barely spoken since they surfaced from the dive.

'Jeez, Remi, I know you're pissed at me taking the plates, but come on, lighten up! It's done.'

'It's not just the plates, it was the whole dive. It-it just felt… weird,' said Remi as he watched Dwight inspect the fingers on his right hand, something he'd noticed him keep doing ever since they were back aboard the boat.

'You always say dives are creepy.'

'Not creepy! They can be eerie. But this was different. It felt wrong as soon as I saw the wreck … and then when we surfaced that squall came up from nowhere. Water was comin' over the sides, then it was a virtual flat calm. It was odd!'

Dwight laughed.

'What're you sayin', Remi? That we're living in an episode of *The Twilight Zone* or somethin'?'

'I'm just sayin' it was strange. And you're damn right, taking those plates doesn't sit well with me.'

'It was my charter, man,' stated Dwight, cruelly emphasising that Remi hadn't been able to afford the dive. Remi shook his head and looked away, and Dwight realised he'd kicked him where it hurt.

'How about I give a couple away?' offered Dwight. 'All three are the same anyway, so how about I give two to Callum as a kinda tip? He'll be in the bar later.'

'Why not give him all three?'

'No way, man! A plate from the *Vanguard* is a real memento,' stated Dwight, before looking at his fingers once again. Remi winced at how loud he was.

'Keep your voice down, man,' said Remi through a tight mouth, 'and don't keep mentioning the *Vanguard*, for God's sake.'

'Come on, Remi,' replied Dwight, more quietly. 'Who's gonna know what we're talkin' about?' He looked around the busy restaurant as he said it as if to confirm his view, noticing an attractive young woman with long chestnut hair at a table by the door. She was scrolling on her phone as she waited for her food, seemingly oblivious to the happy hubbub of the restaurant around her.

Laura Matson studiously looked down as if absorbed by the content on the small screen in her hand. In reality, she'd managed to look away before the loud American had caught her eye. Though she wasn't close enough to hear the conversation he was having with his friend, their expressions and tone suggested some tension between them. It had clearly followed on from when they'd walked past her along the waterfront of Pier Road, where she'd spent the afternoon painting a watercolour. She remembered how they'd been straight-faced and silent as they trudged past, like an old married couple gripped by a festering quarrel. It was also evident they were divers. They'd landed from a small boat, on which she had recognised the ginger hair and stocky frame of Callum Craigie, who was lugging air tanks around the deck after they'd disembarked.

On Laura's phone was a screenshot of the picture she'd created earlier. It was a waterside view of the inlet at St Margaret's Hope and the hills beyond on a rare, calm day, depicting glittering water and distant green uplands under benign shades of blue. She smiled at the thumbs-up emoji her mum had sent back after Laura had forwarded the image to her. It was something Laura did with all her paintings, just as her mum always replied with a thumbs-up or "lovely". Though she could be overly critical of her own work, Laura was quietly pleased with this one, feeling it captured something of the place she now called home. It was certainly a picture she thought might sell, hence why she was treating herself to a rare meal out.

She took a sip of white wine and sneaked a look at the Americans who were now eating their desserts quietly. Though she'd not been eavesdropping, Laura had heard the word "Vanguard" a couple of times and wondered what it meant. She'd thought of asking Callum, who would probably be in the bar later. Then again, she didn't want to seem too enthusiastic. Laura had met Callum in Murray's, as the locals called it, where he'd made it clear he was interested in her. Given that he was only nineteen, ten years her junior, and they had little in common other than living in the same village, neighbourly friendship was her limit with Callum – though awkwardly, he didn't seem to have received that message yet.

Laura looked up and smiled as the waitress delivered her seafood tagliatelle. She noticed she wasn't the only single diner in the room. At a table next to the bar, an unremarkable balding man, probably in his late middle age, stared into a half empty beer glass. The small scene reeked of loneliness.

Alan Muir was wrestling with himself over whether to order a second beer despite having to drive back to Kirkwall when the sight of two of his parishioners arriving in the restaurant ended his inner discussion. They smiled warmly on spotting him and he reciprocated with a wave and a grin that slipped from his face once the couple were seated and their heads buried in menus.

The restaurant was a happy hive of chatter. Yet Alan felt empty and, having looked forward to some lovely seafood all day, he now wished he hadn't come. The sight of couples or groups of friends talking and laughing emphasised how much he was alone just as much as spending another night in front of the television. At least on the sofa he could always anaesthetise himself with another drink. Here, particularly mindful of the fact he was a priest, he knew a second Red McGregor would be noticed. Orkney was a very small place, after all. And what did the fact he felt the need for another beer – or, better still, a large single malt – say about him? Was it really a healthy mindset for a supposed man of God? As he sank the last of his beer, Alan mused that "supposed" was the only part of that question he was currently certain of.

Laura looked up at the scraping of a chair followed by the big American's loud, jarring voice.

'C'mon, Remi, it's our last night. Let's hit the bar!' announced Dwight, leaving his chair askew and striding towards the inner door.

The smaller American thanked the waitress, placed both chairs under the table, then smiled apologetically at Laura on his way out. She smiled back, then looked in the direction of the bar, where Dwight had disappeared to, and raised an eyebrow. Nothing needed to be said. Remi's eyes crinkled knowingly and his mouth formed into a wry line.

It was proving to be a typical Friday night at The Murray Arms. By the time Dwight and Remi had made their way from the restaurant to the bar, it was standing room only. They squeezed into a pocket of space on the right and Remi noticed Callum sat on a bench by the window, laughing loudly with a couple of friends, their table laden with bottles. He nodded to Callum just as Dwight spotted him while turning back from the bar with two pint glasses.

'Hey, Callum. I'll get you a Skull Splitter,' shouted Dwight, beckoning him over.

Callum rose a little unsteadily as the effects of the beer made their presence felt and he moved clumsily through the throng towards Dwight and Remi.

'I've got something for you, bro,' said Dwight. He handed Callum a Skull Splitter then made to leave the room. 'Just gimme a minute. It's upstairs.'

As Dwight departed, Remi raised a glass to Callum, who reciprocated with his latest bottle of strong ale.

'Thanks for the trip earlier, Callum,' said Remi. Then he lowered his voice and leant in close, asking, 'You ever had that sort of localised swell before?'

Callum was happily half-cut but a shadow crossed his features at the memory of being tossed inexplicably in that angry patch of sea. He shook his head as Dwight burst back in with a carrier bag, scrunched over at the top, its contents hidden.

'Remi and I want you to have this as a token of our appreciation,' schmoozed Dwight.

As soon as Callum took the bag, he realised what was inside. He also knew he didn't want the plates, but he could hardly refuse. He managed to offer his thanks with a polite nod, though Remi sensed his uncertainty.

'They're yours to do what you will with. Maybe sell to an antique shop?' said Remi.

Callum nodded again, then Dwight tried to talk out of the side of his mouth.

'Just don't say where they came from, eh, buddy?'

'I'm no' fuckin' stupid!' snapped Callum uncharacteristically, the beer starting to talk.

Remi winced. Dwight was not a man to let such a comment ride, but before he could respond, a woman with a mop of grey hair and dark, intense eyes was in front of him.

'Excuse me, but could I please speak with you outside?' she asked in a local accent.

'What for?' asked Dwight.

She was middle-aged and wearing a hairy green cardigan – hardly his type. 'Please?' she added.

'OK, lady. It'd better be good,' replied Dwight as they squeezed through the throng to the door.

After Laura had eaten, she stepped through the glass doors of the restaurant with the remains of her wine to satisfy her craving for a cigarette. She knew it was a bad habit she'd developed, smoking each time she drank, but she had convinced herself it was OK the few nights a week that she went to the pub. It had started last year during her first long Orkney winter, a time when she was still reeling from her flight from Matthew, from London and from her job as an art teacher. It was a lonely, confusing period when a drink in a warm, welcoming pub was like a salve for a damaged soul, and she'd started joining a few others for a social fag outside as the evening wore on. Tonight she stood quietly, savouring the tang of the cigarette, alone but quite content.

Laura then noticed the loud American from the restaurant who was now in the company of a woman she recognised as a local. They faced each other closely and though he was much taller, the woman's upward gaze was fearlessly direct.

'I understand this seems a wee bit strange, but I need to tell you what I saw,' said the woman, her face showing concern.

'What you saw?'

'I saw a figure behind you when you came into the bar,' she said.

'What are you talking about?' asked Dwight, irritated and off balance.

'The ghost of a sailor was looking over your shoulder when you passed that bag to young Callum.'

For a few moments Dwight looked around him, agitated, his mouth working soundlessly. Then he exploded.

'What bullshit is this? And who are you, trying to scare me with some crazy ghost stuff?'

'I'm Shona Drever. I live here in St Margaret's Hope. I see the dead and that's the truth, whether you believe me or not,' she said evenly.

'Get the fuck away from me!' shouted Dwight. The courtyard fell silent and all eyes locked on him.

Laura jumped at Dwight's volume and venom. It took her back to the Camden flat and how Matthew could cow and control with his voice. Unconsciously, she stepped further away from Dwight, almost into the shadows, as if to hide herself.

Alan Muir was stepping out of the restaurant when he heard Dwight and saw the agitation in his body language. As others were suddenly quiet and watchful, Alan moved quickly forward, nodded politely at Shona, smiled at the American and positioned himself slightly between them.

'Excuse me, sir, is everything OK?' asked Alan calmly.

'What's it to you?' snapped Dwight.

'It's just that I could see you were upset. How about we take a seat?'

'I'll repeat, what's it to you?' Dwight said, louder now, leaning over Alan as he boiled up even more. Alan held his gaze, an easy half-smile on his face.

'Well, as a priest, it's important I don't walk past when there's upset. I'm Alan Muir, by the way,' he said evenly, unperturbed.

That one word, priest, melted Dwight's hot temper. While he no longer believed in God, Dwight's Catholic upbringing meant some ties still held firm, though he couldn't explain why. One of those was a simple reverence for the ordained. Dwight's shoulders dropped and he nodded respectfully before shaking Alan's hand. He then looked at Shona ruefully and said a very quiet "sorry", which Laura was able to lip-read. Shona smiled in return, nodded gratefully at Alan, then walked away towards Pier Road as the two men engaged briefly in some jocular small talk.

Intrigued and impressed by the older man's intervention, Laura hovered in the background and, when

Dwight returned inside smiling following a pat on the back and a cheery word from Alan, she did what she normally didn't by stepping forwards and introducing herself.

'Hello, I'm Laura and… er… I just wanted to say thank you.'

'Hello, Laura. I'm Alan. Though I don't know why you're thanking me,' he replied in a strong Edinburgh burr, his kind blue eyes creasing as he smiled.

'For stopping that awful scene. That guy was getting aggressive and a bit scary.'

Alan shrugged. 'I've seen a lot worse,' he said. 'I used to lead a church near Glasgow. Orkney's easier, even if you throw in the occasional angry American.'

Laura laughed before being lost for words.

'Well… thanks again,' she offered awkwardly.

'No problem. Goodnight, now. Take care,' Alan said, before walking to a black Focus, pleased to have been of use and happy that someone had acknowledged it.

Laura was not religious. If anything, she would say she was an atheist and had no time for "God-botherers", as her dad always called such people. Yet there was something about Alan Muir…

Her chain of thought snapped when Callum appeared with a carrier bag.

'There's something in there for you,' he said.

'What?'

'Have a look and find out. There's one for you and one for me,' he slurred.

As soon as she saw the plate, she didn't like it, though she couldn't have explained why.

'What is it?'

'It's a mess plate. Sailors used them on ships. The divers found them just scanning the seabed today.'

'It's not from a wreck, is it?' asked Laura.

'It might be, but not one o' the known wrecks, no. Ye can't take stuff from them without permission,' announced Callum.

'I'm not sure, Callum. I—'

'Go on, have it. If ye don't want to keep it, sell it on or somethin',' said Callum, suddenly distracted by a passing friend who he turned towards, laughing.

As Laura watched Callum clowning drunkenly with his pal, she put the plate down on a bench. She was on edge; maybe the row earlier had set her off. Whatever the cause, she suddenly wanted to go home. She went to leave, but when she was barely ten yards from the door, Callum called after her. Her heart sank.

'Here, Laura, ye've left yer plate. Here, take it.'

3

Dougie MacKay climbed into the seat of his rusting Land Cruiser a little unsteadily just as the evening rain began to speckle his coat. It was exactly ten o'clock, his usual getaway time from the Hoy Hotel, where he enjoyed a dram or two most evenings. Dougie was probably over the limit, but he never worried about that. The farmhouse was only two miles away and there was rarely anyone on Hoy's roads at night anyway. The engine spluttered a little before settling into a steady thrum as he put the news on the radio and pulled on to the road out of Lyness, his lights soon spearing through the rainy night.

Suddenly, shadowy figures ran across the road. They were so close that Dougie braked and swerved left, his nearside wheels biting into the grass verge, spinning him sideways before he lurched forwards as the engine stalled.

He opened his rain-smeared window to see where they had run to but saw no one. They'd somehow melted into the darkness. As he looked back through the windscreen, he realised with a shiver where he was. His headlight beams pointed off the road into Lyness Military Cemetery. The lights illuminated the Celtic memorial cross for those lost on *HMS Vanguard*.

Although Dougie had drunk three generous whiskies, he would swear on the Bible that the three running figures that caused him to lose control had been in sailor's uniform.

Laura padded through to the kitchen in her pyjamas to pour a glass of water. She was not much of a drinker and the two large glasses of wine she'd had earlier had left her ready for an early night.

The plate Callum had given her sat on the kitchen table next to the watercolours she'd done that day. As she looked at it, she wondered where it had come from and what might have become of the people who'd used it. She had no sense of how old it might be, though she did know Scapa Flow had been a naval base in both wars. Maybe the plate was even older and dated from the eighteenth or nineteenth century.

However old it was, she'd decided to take it to an antique shop in Stromness the next day and donate any proceeds to the Refuge charity. After all, Refuge had done so much to support her after she left Matthew. While Laura would be the first to credit her dear old parents for their financial help in enabling her to escape to Orkney and start anew, it was the people at Refuge that understood her and made her feel justified in walking away.

As Laura filled her glass, the rain thrummed on the window as if she needed a reminder as to exactly how far she had "walked away". Camden to Orkney was certainly some move, one she'd questioned many times when the wind howled, the rain seemed incessant and she had very little money coming in. At such times, Laura would remind herself of the plan – to be a world away from Matthew, where she could paint and answer the question she'd always harboured: could she make a living as an artist?

Her parents had certainly given her the opportunity. She'd cried when her mum had offered to give her fifty thousand pounds, saying that she'd get it all at some point and this seemed as good a time as any to help her out. They had then, understandably, been taken aback when she explained she was renting a bungalow in Orkney for a year to go and paint. Other than a few trusted friends, her parents were the only people who knew where she'd gone. One year had become two when Laura started to sell some of her work and her earnings matched her outgoings. So, Laura had committed to a third year in the hope of actually making a living and not just hiding and healing in this bare, beautiful landscape.

Callum Craigie swayed away from The Murray Arms with the remaining mess plate in a carrier bag. It had been his usual Friday skinful, made better by the fact that Saturday was the second of the two days he'd booked off work. He was being soaked by the rain, but it was only a short walk to the family home on Front Road where his bedroom overlooked the sea.

Callum had talked to friends about getting his own place in Stromness nearer work, but the truth was he liked living at home. His rent was cheap and his mum still looked after him. He'd realised this the year before when he stayed in an apartment in Greece for two weeks with four mates. The washing had soon built up, the place became filthy and their money ran out.

As Callum approached the door, fishing clumsily in his jeans pocket for his keys, he remembered the plate in the wet, flapping carrier bag. He didn't want any awkward questions about it from his parents, so he unlocked his car and put the bag in the rear footwell before stabbing his key in the lock, thumping up the stairs and crashing on to the bed fully clothed. Callum was wet and he still had his trainers on, but the beer had done its work and he was snoring within two minutes.

Remi woke at Dwight's cry. He clicked the side light on and blinked in the sudden brightness. Dwight stared at him through puffy, red-rimmed eyes as he lay on his back. The duvet wrapped around him as if he'd been wrestling with it.

'You called out. Are you OK?' asked Remi, noticing the sweat sticking Dwight's blond hair to his forehead. He could also see his chest heaving under his t-shirt.

'Uh, a little restless, if I'm honest, man,' admitted Dwight.

He looked more than a little restless to Remi.

'You look like shit,' said Remi.

'Well, it's three in the morning and I had a few beers more than I should've.'

Dwight stomped to the bathroom, where Remi could hear him cough, relieve himself, fart noisily and run the tap, before returning to his bed. What Remi couldn't know was that Dwight's heart was racing and his mind was starting to do the same.

In fact, Dwight was worried about going back to sleep. He'd dreamt about diving on the wreck. After pulling the first mess plate out, he was reaching for the second when a hand emerged in a flurry of blinding silt and grabbed his wrist. He had to use all his strength to resist it but he could feel the large, strong hand pressing into his wrist as he began to tire. He was being pulled inexorably downwards when Remi put the light on.

Dwight was also thinking about the finger he'd hurt when retrieving the plates. It still tingled, yet there was no mark, no remains of a sea urchin's spine, nothing. He decided to get it checked as soon as he was back in New York.

He could hear a slow drip from somewhere, which was also annoying him. Rain had clearly found its way in, but he was just too tired to move and investigate the leak.

Next to Dwight, the mess plate sat on his bedside locker, slowly filling with dripping water, yet the ceiling above was dry.

Laura was between sleep and wakefulness, her senses muffled, before she gradually attuned to the sound of banging and woke up, alert and fearful.

She sat up to listen. It was loud, regular and, worryingly, sounded like it was inside. Laura's rented property was like many on Orkney, a small, modern bungalow with rooms running off a central corridor. The two bedrooms were at one end, the lounge at the other and the kitchen-diner mid-way, opposite the bathroom. As she came out of her bedroom and reached for the hall light switch, her bare feet slipped on the wooden flooring and she almost fell. When the light came on, her stomach lurched at the sight before her. There were wet footprints in the hall.

Laura froze at first, before switching the hall light off, creeping back into the bedroom, putting a chair under the handle as quietly as she could, then grabbing her phone off the dressing table. She paused, thumbs hovering over the screen. *Would 999 summon the police quickly enough to deal with an intruder? Probably not. How about ringing Callum? He was only a couple of streets away, after all, yet given his usual Friday night session, he'd probably be dead to the world at this hour.*

As she wrestled with what to do, the rhythmic banging continued. Laura wondered why someone who was there either to harm her or burgle the house would draw attention to themselves by making a lot of noise. She put the phone down and looked round for a weapon. The only thing to hand was a tennis racket, but it was at least something. Heart thumping, she moved the chair, opened the door slowly, clicked the light on and moved slowly down the hall, her feet becoming wetter with every measured step. As she neared the kitchen, the noise grew louder. It sounded like the back door was open and banging in the wind. Laura took a deep breath, opened the door and scrabbled for the kitchen light.

The kitchen was empty but the back door was ajar, swinging inwards like an unanswered question. The banging had stopped, and all Laura could hear was her own ragged breathing and the loud tick of the wall clock. She went tentatively to the door, closed it and quickly turned the key. Then she looked out into the small garden, though she couldn't see anything in the darkness. She briefly closed her eyes in relief when she realised the floor was wet right up to the door, as if somebody had walked in or out with wet shoes, but then thought it odd that there was no mud or grit.

She went through the house, turning on the lights and checking each room. She even looked in all the cupboards and under the beds before ringing 999 to report a break-in. It was a massive relief to hear the operator say the police would be with her inside twenty minutes.

Laura was a little calmer after the call, coupled with knowing for certain there was no one in the house. She decided to make a coffee while she waited for the police. It would wake her up but she couldn't envisage getting back to sleep after this episode anyway.

After putting the kettle on, she looked across at her painting from yesterday, which now seemed a very long time ago, before her gaze fell on the mess plate. Laura stopped, then moved to the table for a closer look. It left her mouth gaping and her brow furrowed in puzzlement. The plate was full of water. There was also a smell in the room that she'd never noticed before, which reminded her of seaweed.

4

David Innes unlocked the Scapa Flow Museum doors, then moved quickly to disable the alarm system as the four other staff filed in behind him, shaking the rain from their coats. Though they'd been caught in a shower as they crossed the car park, there were enough patches of blue to suggest it would be a changeable rather than an interminably wet day, and they were hopeful that the first ferry from the mainland would disgorge a healthy number of visitors to the museum, literally a minute's drive from Hoy's Lyness Dock.

David's character was as solid as his rugby player's frame. He was a young man who loved the naval history of Scapa Flow and had found his niche as manager of the museum dedicated to it.

Once the staff had been briefed, David started his pre-opening check of the galleries, switching on lights and power for the interactive displays and working machinery. All seemed in order until he reached the glass exhibition case for *HMS Vanguard*, where he stopped and put his hand contemplatively to his dark, bearded chin. David's peripheral vision had noticed that something wasn't quite right. When he looked closer, his eyebrows knitted in puzzlement.

Some of the artefacts in the cabinet had been moved. A brass ashtray had swapped places with a cigarette box and a vase was now where a lens from a lamp should have resided. The lamp lens now sat on top of a padlock for a sailor's kit bag.

David used his walkie talkie to summon Katie Thomson, the deputy manager. As he was waiting, he noticed there were small patches of water on the floor next to the display. He looked up but couldn't see any leaks. Besides, it was raining now, yet no water was dripping down.

'You called, my lord!' chirped Katie with a smile from beneath her mop of auburn curls.

David uncharacteristically ignored her simple jest, his frown remaining in place.

'What do you make of this?'

Katie looked at the display, immediately seeing that some items had been moved before identifying exactly what had changed.

'Who would jumble stuff up like that?' she asked, looking perplexed.

David shrugged, then pointed at the patches of water.

'And what do you make of that? It's raining now and

there's no dripping from the roof. The floor's level, too. So where's it come from?'

'Could the CCTV help?'

'It shows the room and the display from the side, but the camera angle's wrong to see inside the case.'

'What about the water?'

'It might show that. I tell you what, you sort the display out and I'll look at the CCTV.'

Alan Muir sat on the front pew of the empty church watching a single candle burn on the white-clothed altar. He had a headache courtesy of too much whisky the night before. While he'd felt alone and miserable during his meal at The Murray Arms, his successful intervention in the rumpus outside left him feeling pleased with himself and he'd enjoyed the journey back to Kirkwall along quiet meandering roads with U2 as an accompaniment. Yet as soon as he'd opened his front door and stepped into the quiet of his house, the loneliness had hit him once again. It wasn't just that *Alison* wasn't there, it was now the fact that *no one* was there again. As it was almost every night. Alan now seemed past the point where prayer helped. He didn't want to hear "the Lord's ways are mysterious" anymore. He wanted answers.

In despair one day, he'd walked alone on the coast and shouted out to sea. He'd screamed at God who, if he was all-powerful, had taken his wife away. He'd raged at the top of his voice for God to at least give him some insight into why Alison had died. He shouted until his voice cracked into a high-pitched whine, then failed, and his last sobbing breaths were carried away on the wind, lost at sea. That's how his prayers felt now, as if they were carried to nowhere. The sad truth was that the Church had become a job, not a calling, and Alan often felt like a fraud.

Laura sat bleary-eyed at the kitchen table with her hands round a coffee, half listening to the radio as the presenter announced the ten a.m. news. She was usually an early riser but was still in her pyjamas after what had been a long, unusual and frightening night.

The police had arrived quickly though. The two young male constables were also reassuringly thorough, checking the whole property, the garden and the surrounding area. They had, however, exchanged a look when she mentioned the plate filling with water despite there being no apparent leak.

Laura felt that they had bracketed her as an arty, mystical type who was highly strung. Their suggestion had been to call a plumber and put a deeper pan on the table in case the water started leaking again. Having spotted the glance between them, she didn't mention the wet footprints or the seaweed smell, which had dissipated by the time they arrived, but she did ask them how someone could have opened the kitchen door when there was clearly no evidence of a forced entry. They offered two possible explanations; firstly, that she hadn't locked the door, which didn't explain how it could swing open; secondly, that someone else had a key – but her landlord was an eighty-five-year-old woman who lived in Kirkwall. The idea that she would drive to the bungalow, pad around in wet footwear, repeatedly bang the door and run away when Laura stirred was preposterous.

Though the lack of an explanation for what had happened was unsettling, the police visit and the onset of daylight meant she didn't feel scared now. She looked at the mess plate, still on the table in front of her. It was an interesting piece and not unattractive, but there was something about it she just didn't like. Though she was artistic and considered herself soulful, Laura also thought of herself as a very rational person, certainly not superstitious or spiritual. Though there was one time at college when she'd become upset over one of her flatmates using tarot cards and left the room, but couldn't explain why. The plate elicited a similar indefinable feeling. Laura resolved that she'd take whatever the antiques centre offered her for it, even give it away if need be, and the thought of moving it on spurred her into heading for the shower.

'Slow down man, for God's sake!' gasped Dwight O'Neil, as he panted up the open, grassy slope towards Marwick Head ten yards behind Remi. A combination of a hangover and a disturbed night had left the big New Yorker trailing behind his diving partner for once. As Remi reached the cliff top, he turned and grinned at Dwight, enjoying his struggle.

'Self-inflicted suffering!' laughed Remi.

'Yeah,' croaked Dwight as he reached him. 'Skull Splitter by name, skull splitter by nature.'

Dwight then took a few more paces to the edge of

the cliff, high above a fierce, roiling sea. The buffeting of the wind, the battering waves far below and the cries of hundreds of sea birds whose nests gave off the sour tang of ammonia was an assault on the senses.

To their left rose the imposing Kitchener's Memorial, like a stone keep standing guard over Orkney's northern coast. They walked around it to the memorial skirting its front that commemorated those lost in the seas in front of them when *HMS Hampshire* had struck a mine in 1915. Both were quiet and thoughtful as they read some of the seven hundred plus names set in the low stone wall, spotting Lord Kitchener's among the long, sad list.

Then they picked up the grassy path back along the cliff, Dwight leading the way before calling back to Remi.

'Y'know, the *Hampshire*'s not far out there and you can reach it with scuba gear,' he said, turning to Remi with a grin.

'Forget it, Dwight. No more illegal diving, y'hear?' replied Remi, shaking his head with a rueful smile, which slipped from his face as Dwight cried out and fell forward.

Dwight's head and shoulders were over the edge of the cliff and his widening eyes could see the foaming sea breaking on the rocks a long way below. Remi dropped to his knees and grabbed his friend's boots. Dwight was a big man and for a second both men thought he might fall, but he was also strong and with Remi anchoring his lower half, he managed to haul himself backwards and away from danger. Remi gave his legs a pull for good measure as Dwight turned on to his back. Once his breath returned, he looked at Remi with a mixture of incredulity and anger.

‘What the fuck are you doing! Is that your idea of a joke? Because I ain’t laughin’. I could o’ died there, man!’

‘I didn’t do anything, Dwight. I was just behind you and saw you fall.’

‘Don’t give me that shit! I felt you trip me from behind.’

‘I never tripped you. I swear.’

Dwight looked into Remi’s eyes. He knew this guy; he knew he was honest. His expression was genuine. As Dwight lay there, his heart thumping, his finger began tingling again and he felt scared. Remi offered him a hand.

‘Come on, Dwight. Let’s get movin’. It’s less than an hour until we check in at the airport. The flight’s at one p.m.’

Dwight nodded and stood up, and they started their short downhill journey across the coarse, grassy track to the hire car. He may have only been walking, but Dwight’s heart and mind were racing.

David Innes sat back in his office chair, chewing his lip in thought as he waited for Katie to join him. As she entered with a smile, he sat forward, hunched over his computer, and patted the seat he’d placed next to his in invitation.

‘Look at this. It’s weird,’ said David as he clicked the play button and the still CCTV image became live.

Katie looked at the dim image of the gallery where the *HMS Vanguard* collection was. As David had said, the angle didn’t afford a view inside the display case, though it did show the floor in front of it. Subconsciously, Katie moved closer to the screen. Her brow furrowed at what she was seeing. Wet marks began to appear, one after the other in sequence. They weren't fully distinct in the gloomy, grainy footage, but it was clear enough to see something was happening.

'What can you see?' asked David, seeking confirmation for what he thought he'd seen.

'It looks like wet footprints. The way one follows another, like step after step.'

'That's what I think too.'

They looked at each other, both incredulous and a little shaken.

'You ever seen anything like this before?' asked Katie, to which David shook his head.

'I've never heard any staff say they've seen anything either, and I've been here a few years now,' replied David.

'What should we do?'

'What can we do? If we say something to staff, it'll freak them out. Let's sleep on it and see if anything else happens.'

Katie bit her lip, considering what David had said, then nodded.

'It's not as if anything dangerous has happened. At least not yet,' she laughed, with a note of nervousness.

5

Callum had finally woken just after eleven a.m., though it was past noon by the time he could face anything to eat. Once his stomach had been settled with tea and toast, he'd showered, grunted to his mother that he'd be back for tea and headed out to his car. The plan was to meet up with some mates in Kirkwall, go for a beer and watch the early match in the pub, then take things from there – a rare lazy Saturday. As he closed the front door, he remembered with a smile the old saying that summed up how he felt on a day off from the dive boats: "nothing to do and all day to do it".

The red Golf's custom exhaust growled loudly as he crawled through the narrow streets of St Margaret's Hope, before roaring up the hill and away towards Kirkwall to the accompaniment of a thumping dance beat.

Callum drove quickly though skilfully, fully focused

on the winding roads, punctuated by the straight sections on the Churchill Barriers built during the last war as permanent blocks against German U-boats. They were now spectacular bridges that linked some of the islands to the mainland. As he drove over Barrier 3, Callum couldn't help but glance right, as he always did, at the striking remains of the SS Reginald, one of the blockships sunk in the First World War, its rusting hull and exposed ribs akin to the carcass of a dead whale beached in the shallows.

Once off the barrier road, he closed quickly on a vehicle he recognised. The old blue Astra in front was Laura Matson's car. *Going slow as usual,* thought Callum. After some sharp, climbing bends, the road opened up and he dropped the Golf into third, accelerated alongside Laura while presenting a gurning face, then sped off, the thumping bass and howling exhaust receding quickly as he disappeared into the distance. Laura smiled to herself, thinking it better to be sure to reach the supermarket in Kirkwall five minutes later than risk going off the road, as Callum seemed happy to do every time she saw him driving.

The mess plate was bubble-wrapped in the boot, ready for delivery to the antique shop later. She'd suddenly thought about it because she could detect the funny seaweed smell again. Laura lowered her front windows but couldn't smell it outside the car. When she raised the windows, there it was again within minutes. What she couldn't detect, though, were the two large wet footprints in the passenger footwell behind her seat.

Callum sniffed and wrinkled his nose at the smell that

suddenly permeated his car, a strong aroma of brine and seaweed. It was like being back on the boat. He felt a little nauseous too, though he put it down to last night's beer. He opened the windows, which seemed to clear it a little. As he took the final bends dropping into Kirkwall, the mess plate shifted slightly in the rear passenger footwell. On the rear driver's side, two wet patches had materialised on the rubber mat.

Remi looked at Dwight, sitting beside him at the back of the small, propeller-driven aircraft as it taxied for take-off to Edinburgh. The big New Yorker was silent, seemingly focused on the whining, whirring propellers as he clutched his rucksack strap. Why he'd felt the need to keep the damned mess plate in his hand luggage was a mystery to Remi. He'd also never seen Dwight look so rough, be so quiet or act so oddly. Firstly, there'd been his funny turn in the night, crying out aloud, then this morning he seemed to have had some sort of meltdown on the cliff, almost falling over the edge then blaming Remi. There was also something in his eyes, a trepidation that Remi hadn't seen before. And he was still fiddling with his right index finger every few minutes.

Laura wheeled her trolley quickly through the supermarket gathering what was required for her lasagne later, having decided to do so before she went to the antique shop. As she reached the top of the drinks aisle, she spotted Alan Muir perusing the whisky.

'Is that for the communion?' asked Laura, a little surprised at her own cheek.

It brought a smile to Alan's face as he put a bottle of Glenfiddich in his basket to keep company with a Hawaiian pizza.

'No, but it is medicinal,' laughed Alan, knowing there was some sad truth in his cliched comment.

'I'm Laura. We met briefly last night.'

'Yes, I remember, at The Murray Arms. There was an agitated American.'

Laura nodded with a chuckle.

'It's Alan, isn't it? Or do I call you Father or Reverend, or something else?' Laura gabbled.

'Alan's just fine.'

Laura nodded again before it all came spilling out.

'Well, it's just that I had a funny experience last night. Later in the night, that is, when I got home. There were wet footprints in the house and the back door was open and banging, yet there was no one there. The police came but found nothing. Then this plate I'd been given had water in it, yet there's no way water could have got in it. Then there was a weird smell at one point, I can only describe it like seaweed, then I smelt it in the car coming over. It's all just… odd.'

Alan had struggled to follow Laura's account and didn't know what to say, so he did what he usually did with troubled parishioners and, with a slight smile, said, 'Why don't we finish up here and get a coffee in town so we can talk properly?'

Within fifteen minutes they were sat opposite each

other in The Old Library, sipping lattes. After a little small talk on their backgrounds, Alan steered the conversation to the matter at hand.

'So you had these wet footprints and a door that seems to have opened by itself?' queried Alan.

'Yes.'

'Does anyone else have a key?'

'Only the landlady, but she's elderly and lives here in Kirkwall. It's a ridiculous idea that she'd pad around in wet shoes then bang the door and clear off in the middle of the night.'

'People do strange things, but it sounds unlikely,' said Alan. 'So, where does this plate fit in?'

'It was given to me as a present last night. A guy I know from The Murray Arms insisted I take it. It's a mess plate from a ship, he said.'

'So your point being that there's never been anything untoward in the house before this plate arrived?'

'Yes, and it had water in it for no reason,' stressed Laura, animated now.

'What do you mean?

'I left it on the table when I went to bed and when I came into the kitchen in the early hours, there was water in it and a funny smell in the room. And I checked the ceiling for leaks. I've booked a plumber for Monday to make sure, but I can see there's no dripping or staining. It's just weird. And, if I'm honest…' She searched for the words and settled on the one that fit best. 'Scary.'

'I can see why it's unsettling, certainly,' said Alan. It felt to him a little weak as soon as he'd spoken.

'Being a priest, have you dealt with things like this before?'

'I've blessed houses where people have felt there's been some presence. I've also met a few people who claimed they were possessed or haunted, but they were usually mentally ill. Oh, and I once referred someone on to a deliverance minister.'

'Deliverance minister?'

'Deliverance is, I suppose, a modern term for exorcism. It's not something I've had direct experience of. I've never seen a ghost or driven out a demon, I'm afraid.'

'So, I suppose I'm just some flaky nutter,' said Laura with a self-deprecating smile, but she was testing the waters, seeing if he believed her.

There was a pause as Alan seemed to weigh Laura's words.

'Where's the plate now?' he asked finally.

'In the boot of my car. I was taking it to an antique shop today.'

'Why not leave it with me for a few days?'

'That's a great idea!' beamed Laura, happy to be rid of it.

Alan smiled in return. *What harm could it do?* he thought.

Remi relaxed back in his seat as the pilot released the brakes and, with a sharp increase in noise, the aircraft built up speed before lifting off. It was a little more gradual than the jets he was used to, but they were soon well clear of the ground and banking left, affording them a fine, clear view. Looking past Dwight, who had the window seat, Remi deduced they were heading south with Scapa Flow directly below them. As Remi spotted the island of Flotta, he knew *HMS Vanguard* was somewhere below the water nearby. Images of their dive to it flooded back and he felt guilty.

Then his thoughts and feelings were dislocated as the aircraft dropped violently. It stabilised for a second, then began yo-yoing and vibrating. It was the worst turbulence Remi had ever encountered. Some passengers cried out in fear. Remi gripped the armrests tightly. He looked round at the flight attendant, thankfully still strapped in behind them. It was disconcerting to see such fear on her face too.

Though it seemed much longer, the turbulence was over in less than thirty seconds. As the aircraft settled into a stable climb, Remi took a deep breath, then glanced at Dwight. Usually, he would have laughed annoyingly during such an episode. Today he was silent and open-mouthed as the captain's disembodied voice filled the cabin, apologising for the unforeseen turbulence and requesting they keep their seatbelts fastened. Remi took another concerned look at his dive buddy, who was staring blankly forwards through tired, frightened eyes. At that moment, one word came into Remi's mind to describe Dwight. He looked haunted.

6

Jean Craigie heard her son Callum's noisy old car long before she saw it pull up outside the house, obscuring her view of Water Sound and the hills of Burray beyond. Lady, their Border Collie, knew the Golf's exhaust note too and she jumped off the sofa and stood by the lounge door with ears pricked and tail wagging as she waited for Callum to step through it. The clock on the mantlepiece showed it was just after four p.m., much earlier than Jean had expected him to return. He'd no doubt soon be on his way again after a few brief words if she was lucky. Not that Jean resented her son's unexplained comings and goings, which resembled those of a hotel guest more than a family member. He was a young man, after all. If he couldn't be carefree on his occasional days off, when could he be?

Callum was so different to Liz, his older sister, a

trainee solicitor in Edinburgh. She'd been a high-flyer at school, always destined for success, whereas Callum struggled academically, lacking motivation in class and preferring practical things. At least he'd found work on the dive boats, which seemed less arduous than being a ferryman like his father Iain. He'd been on the St Margaret's Hope to Gills Bay route for years, crossing the predictably unpredictable waters of the Pentland Firth most days. While Jean was proud that they both earned an honest living in Orkney's challenging waters, she also wished they had easier, safer jobs. In Orkney, though, relatively comfortable, well-paid employment was hard to come by and Jean was grateful that with her work at the supermarket in Kirkwall on top of Iain's regular wage, they had a good, if modest, living.

Yet she worried about Callum. He'd always been a loving, decent lad at heart, but she also knew he could be impulsive and easily led. He'd also developed a real taste for drink, but swore he didn't when driving and promised her he'd never touch drugs, a growing issue even on Orkney. All she could do was trust him, but it didn't stop her fretting.

'Hiya,' said Callum as he entered the room, before throwing himself down on to the sofa and Lady began jumping excitedly on him, licking at his face.

'You're back early,' said Jean.

'Aye, only Gary turned up to the pub. Ally and Jack were playin' football at the Picky. We're all meeting in Kirkwall tonight instead.'

'So you'll want feedin' then?' smiled Jean.

'Aye,' yawned Callum as he stroked Lady, who had curled up next to him, her head in his lap.

'Well, yer dad's not back in 'til gone eight, but I've put a casserole on so ye' can have some o' that. It'll be ready for six.'

'Sounds good. I'll take Lady down to Hoxa for a run first,' said Callum. He stood up and Lady curled around his legs, her tail whipping back and forth in anticipation.

Once in the hall, Callum took the lead from a coat peg and picked up his keys from the table before stepping out to the car. He clicked the key fob and opened the back door for Lady to jump on to the blanket that was kept on the back seat for her, but she stopped, sniffed inside the car and turned back to the house with her tail between her legs.

'Come on, girl, in we go!' urged Callum.

Lady just looked at him from the doorstep with wary eyes and her ears submissively flat. Callum knew she was frightened but couldn't see why. She loved going in the car. Then he noticed the plate in its red carrier bag in the footwell. *Maybe it smells funny,* thought Callum. He'd noticed that briny smell earlier. It could be that Lady just didn't like it.

Callum removed the plate, opened the front door and placed it on the lower shelf of the hall table. Lady watched him closely, then turned and jumped into the rear of the car before looking expectantly at Callum as if to say, *Where are we going then?* Callum shook his head, climbed into the car and started it up, ready to take Lady to Hoxa Head, where they could walk through the deserted wartime gun positions hugging the cliffs. As Callum roared up the slope and out of the village with Lady's lolling tongue over his shoulder, he was hoping there were no sheep so she could run free while he enjoyed the views over the water to Hoy.

Edinburgh Airport was alive with people, bustling to the departure gates or sitting by them looking bored, impatient or both. Remi was both, as well as uncomfortable, as they sat on the hard metal seats near gate seven. The constant background noise made reading difficult and he found listening to music through his smartphone at such times odd, his preferred R&B sounds incongruous with the hectic surroundings.

At least Dwight appeared to have relaxed since the flight from Orkney. He was snoring gently, his eyes closed and his head tilted to one side. It was something Remi had seen him do at airports before and he was envious of Dwight's ability to seemingly unplug from the world and sleep when there was nothing much else to do.

However, if Remi could have inhabited Dwight's dream, there would be no envy. For Dwight was back diving on the wreck of *HMS Vanguard*, swimming above the debris field where the middle of the ship had been, surveying her tangled, rusting remains once again. He spotted the porthole with the cracked glass and moved close to it, looking to see his reflection in it using his torch. Yet he couldn't quite seem to see himself in the refracted glass, so went closer still, until he was within a foot of the porthole. As he lined up above it, he gagged in shock as a young man's face stared back at him, as if he had somehow been lying in wait underneath it. He mouthed angrily at Dwight as two tattooed arms emerged from the seabed in a spray of blinding silt, grabbing his shoulders. They were strong arms, too strong to break free from, and Dwight felt himself pulled irresistibly down. As he hit the bottom, his respirator was torn roughly away, breaking his teeth. Salty water and crunchy silt filled his mouth and he began to choke and drown in the darkness.

Remi touched Dwight's arm when he cried out, a frightened, anguished cry like the night before. Dwight blinked awake and his eyes looked around wildly as he gasped for breath.

'Hey, Dwight, you're OK.'

But Dwight was not OK. He pushed Remi away as if he was a would-be assassin and looked around, panting and confused, trying to process where he was and what was happening as he breathed ever faster. Remi gave him room as a young Scottish woman came forwards from the seats opposite.

'He's having a panic attack,' she said authoritatively, then moved closer, slowly taking Dwight's hand before getting him to focus on her as she spoke calmly, telling him she was a doctor and to do as she asked. Within a couple of minutes, she had skilfully regulated Dwight's breathing and he sat quietly, his brow beaded in sweat. He looked as if he had just run a marathon.

The doctor asked Remi to fetch some water. On his return, she confirmed that Dwight had woken from a nightmare. When Remi asked what it was about, Dwight quickly spoke for himself.

'It was nothing. Just some weird dream. I didn't know where I was when I woke, so I freaked a bit.'

Remi nodded but looked dubious.

'Honestly, man, I'm good,' said Dwight with a weak smile, though Remi noticed how he was touching his finger again. He still had the mess plate in the rucksack on his lap like he was guarding the crown jewels.

Callum knew he was in some sort of trouble as soon as he walked into the lounge. His mother, Jean, was sat with her arms folded and his auntie, Shona, Jean's older sister, was in the chair by the window. Both had their mouths set in a tight line and he withered under their glare as Lady jumped up next to Jean and curled into a furry ball, clearly sensing the mood and quickly switching allegiance.

'What?' asked Callum.

'Where did that plate come from?' snapped Jean.

'Why? What's the problem?'

'I don't like it. I don't want it in the house,' said Jean.

'I can sense a presence attached to it, Callum,' added Shona.

'Oh, not this ghost shite again, Auntie Shona!'

'Hey! Language, ma lad!' shouted Jean.

'Sorry, Ma, but all this talk o' spirits, it gives me the creeps.'

'It's real, Callum, whether you like it or not,' said Shona.

Callum shook his head and pulled a face. 'So the plate's haunted then. Is that it?' he sneered.

'I can just feel there's a presence, Callum, an unhappy presence, like it's been disturbed. I can feel it and I can smell it. I think it's off a ship and that's why I saw the sailor last night.'

'What sailor?' asked Callum.

'The one I saw behind that big-mouthed Yank in the pub last night when he gave you those plates.'

'But there were no sailors in there,' said Callum.

'It was a ghost, Callum. He was looking over the American's shoulder when he passed the plates over in the bag.'

Callum didn't know what to say. He thought Auntie Shona was a bit strange with her spiritualist stuff, but how did she come up with the idea of seeing a sailor and link it with the plates coming off a ship?

'If it makes ye' feel better, I'll put the plate in the car,' was all he could offer in reply.

'What're you going to do with it?' asked Shona, clearly concerned.

'And ye've still not said where it's from, ma lad!' added Jean.

'All I know is that the Yanks gave it me as a tip. They'd been divin' from our boat,' offered Callum, but his mother and auntie looked dubious.

Callum retreated from their synchronised glares into the hall to retrieve the plate and put it in the car. He then went straight upstairs, deciding to lie low in his bedroom until tea was ready before heading out straight after eating to Kirkwall, where he'd speak to Ross Tweddle. Ross was a well-known fence with contacts in Thurso and Wick. He could probably get rid of the plate, hopefully for a decent amount too.

7

Laura searched methodically through the house one room at a time, checking they were empty and all of the windows were locked. It was something she'd done religiously on first moving to Orkney, frightened that Matthew would track her down. As the months passed, she gradually lowered her guard to the point where she only checked the outside doors, but the disturbances of the previous night had awakened dormant worries.

It meant the knife block would be going back under the bed tonight, and probably tomorrow too. As she lifted it, the same block she'd had in London, the image of Matthew's face twisted in rage as he pointed the bread knife at her was in her mind once again. She couldn't remember his threats word for word now, but the menacing shout, the glint of the blade and the angry, malevolent expression remained vivid and raw, stamped indelibly like a searing brand. Laura shook her head as if it would clear the images, then walked through to the bedroom, placing the knife block next to the bedside locker.

As she padded back to the kitchen, she decided to open a bottle of merlot, poured a large quantity into one of the bigger glasses with a satisfying glug and retired to the lounge, thinking some TV would be a good distraction. After flicking through a few channels, she settled on a documentary about Britpop, the soundtrack to her early childhood. It absorbed her attention until Oasis loomed on to the screen, performing "Don't Look Back in Anger".

It took her straight back to the sobbing car journey she'd made once Matthew had gone for a bath, acting as if nothing had happened. As she'd turned the key in her Astra, Oasis had burst out of the speakers and with a thumping heart and tear-brimmed eyes, she had sung aloud "Don't Look Back in Anger", her voice cracking as she drove away from the flat for the last time.

It had been only a short journey to Keisha's, but once inside her house it felt as if she was in another country. Keisha, her head of department, and her husband, Tremaine, had been so kind; listening, putting her up until she found a new flat, and encouraging her to speak to Refuge.

Tremaine had even gone back to Laura's flat with his brother, Tommy, to collect her things. Although Matthew's texted reply had been challenging when Laura had informed him they were coming, he had acquiesced meekly once they arrived, given that Tremaine was six feet four and his brother was similarly built.

"Don't Look Back in Anger" still evoked powerful memories, but as Liam Gallagher sang the final lines, seemingly chewing the microphone, Laura recalled what Keisha had said to her on her last day of teaching: 'Remembering, however horrible, means surviving.'

So, as Jarvis Cocker began jumping to the beat of "Common People", Laura took a large gulp of wine and smiled. Yes, she was scarred, sometimes still scared, but she was in Orkney doing what she loved. It was certainly a lot more than just surviving. Oddly, while she still felt uneasy after last night's strangeness, she wasn't terrified.

Callum cupped his ear and leant in close to Ross Tweddle so he could hear him despite the thumping beat in Mambo, a Kirkwall nightspot that was a regular haunt for Callum and his friends.

'So what're ye selling?' asked Ross, before taking a slug from his bottle of Moretti.

'A mess plate,' shouted Callum, looking round in the neon half-light to make sure he wasn't being overheard.

'What the fuck's a mess plate?'

'It's off a ship. The sailors ate off them,' replied Callum.

'Why's it called a mess plate then?'

'Because the sailors were in groups. Each group was called a mess. Each mess had its own stuff, like plates 'n' cups, and they're numbered so they knew which mess they belonged to.'

'Where'd ye get it?'

'All I can say is it came out o' Scapa Flow and it's First World War.'

Ross took another sip, sucked his lip in thought, then said, 'I know someone in Wick who'd be interested, but it'd probably fetch more if he knew where it's from.'

'Let's see what they might pay first. When can you speak to them?' asked Callum.

'Late morning tomorrow when I know they're up an' about. I'll call you when I know something.'

Callum smiled, nodded and clinked his bottle against Ross's Moretti, then turned his attention to a nearby group of girls he'd not seen before with big, drink-fuelled voices and tight, tiny clothes.

Alan Muir swirled the amber dregs of his single malt around the crystal tumbler. It was a tired swirl, out of time with the jaunty strains of Match of the Day, as he contemplated a top-up. It would be his third. He'd left the bottle in the kitchen to avoid the old trap he'd been falling into of having the bottle at his side, leaving him regretting it in the morning. He had a service tomorrow, after all, and had told himself two glasses tonight would be his limit. Yet here he was, thinking about a third, wrestling with himself over a drink once again.

Alan knew he had a problem. It had developed as he struggled through lonely evenings, particularly since coming to Orkney with its long, dark winter nights. When the grief flooded over him, whisky had become his medicine, though now the treatment seemed more damaging than the pain. For a while he had denied it to himself. After all, he didn't wake wanting a drink or stagger around in the daytime like some people he'd tried to help back in Glasgow. He was still functioning and fulfilling his clerical duties, albeit hungover on occasion.

Of late, though, the warning signs were flashing ever more starkly. He was buying whisky from shops in rotation and taking the empties to different bottle banks. Then, last week he had failed to answer a parishioner's late call because he knew he would be slurring, before subsequently lying to her that he'd been asleep when she rang.

There was also the nightly conversation with himself, now stuck on repeat. He'd start most evenings aiming not to have any alcohol that night before the reality of another evening alone bit into his resolve and he told himself one drink was fine. Invariably, one led to two and sometimes considerably more. It all added up to two bottles a week now, and he'd been horrified to realise this was four times the government's recommended amount when he'd read a newspaper article about alcohol abuse.

Alan knew he couldn't go on like this. While he was sober in the day, he often felt rough in the mornings and wondered if his parishioners suspected it. More than anything, he was ashamed. He often reflected on what Alison would think about how he was living; falling asleep in front of the television addled with drink after another Chinese takeaway, then each morning putting on a dog collar and a smiling mask.

He knew that the sensible thing to do would be to see his GP. But how could he when she was a parishioner? How would he look her in the eye again? He'd prayed about it over and again. Given the situation he was in, it felt like he may as well have banged his head against a wall. As he rose unsteadily from his chair to seek out the bottle, he promised himself he wouldn't buy any whisky next week. *Go cold turkey. Others managed it; why not him? But not just now. He could make a fresh start tomorrow.*

Jean Craigie's phone pinged on the arm of the sofa as she half-watched, half-dozed through a an American romcom while her husband, Iain, snored in the chair. The green notification showed it was a text from Callum. Given that it was late – eleven fifteen p.m. – she would have placed good money on what it said.

Hi Ma. I'm staying at Jack's tonight. See you tomorrow morning.

Jean smiled as she read it, having been right again. Callum was staying at his friend Jack Bremner's, as he often did on Saturdays. He'd probably had a few drinks or met a girl, or quite possibly both.

Dwight looked at Remi dozing in the seat to his right, a blue airline blanket over him. The plane was mid-Atlantic and, given the late hour, was quiet in the subdued lighting. Dwight felt something unusual for him: jealousy. At that moment he envied Remi's peace, his ability to sleep and be calm. Because Dwight was far from calm. He was tired, wearily so after such a long day, which now involved a second flight. He so much wanted to put his head back, close his eyes and drift away, like so many of the people on the flight. Just like Remi had done. But he was scared to sleep, frightened of what world he might enter.

He never had bad dreams, but last night and then at the airport, he'd had nightmares. Heart-thumping, horrible nightmares of the *Vanguard* wreck that led to a panic attack. *A panic attack, for God's sake! In public too, with people, including his buddy, looking at him like he was some kind of victim. That happened to flakes and wimps, not to Dwight O'Neil.*

He didn't do scared or nervous. He remembered the butterflies before a big college football game, but that was excitement. The only time he could think of being scared was when he was robbed at gunpoint by two punks on the New York subway, but that fear seemed reasonable. Not wanting to sleep because you were frightened of dreaming wasn't. It was freakin' weird. Period.

He was jittery too and kept sighing, taking an extra deep breath every few minutes. There was also a slight tremor in his hands and his right index finger had now gone dead. The tingling had stopped, but it was numb and would only partially bend. *It all went back to when he'd picked up the mess plates. It must have been some kind of sea urchin or something and he just couldn't see the puncture wound. Hopefully, Doctor Kominsky would find it next week and fix it.*

Or was it something more sinister? Something linked to the kooky woman at The Murray Arms who said there was a ghost behind him? No! That was a crock of shit. Ghosts weren't real. All that after-life garbage was for weirdos. He wasn't giving in to that. He just needed to stop scaring himself.

The mess plate was a find that he would add to his collection, a piece of history to talk about; an artefact that had survived an explosion so big it sank a battleship. Dwight took another deep breath, then quietly said to himself, 'Fuck it, I'm gettin' some sleep.' His mind had been racing and suddenly seemed to reach overload. It shut down like a mental circuit-breaker and Dwight was soon lightly snoring in a deep, dreamless sleep.

Alan's eyes closed and his head lolled forwards as he began to doze to the accompaniment of the commentary of the football and the noise from the crowd. Then he was pulled back to consciousness by a strange and different sound: raucous male singing. Not the cultured tones of a choir, but the strong, rough voices of ordinary men. It was reminiscent of post-rugby match singsongs when he was in the RAF. He opened sticky eyelids to see that Arsenal and Liverpool were still on the television, but the sound was largely drowned by the singing. Alan looked at his watch. It was eleven twenty-one p.m. – an odd time for singing, unless they were drunks?

Alan stood groggily and walked stiffly to the window to see where the singers were. Yet when he poked his head between the curtains and looked out, he saw no one. He even opened the window but there was no singing outside. Curiously, when he shut it again, he could still hear the voices clearly, almost as if they were inside the house.

As soon as Alan opened the lounge door, the singing sounded louder. Was a radio on somewhere? He walked down the long hall dividing the bungalow and the voices grew in volume with every tentative step. They seemed to come from the end room he used as a study. He paused outside the door, now able to make out the tune and words to "Heart of Oak". It sounded as if there was actually a group of men in the room.

'Heart of oak are our ships, heart of oak are our men…'

Alan opened the door and quickly switched the light on, only to be greeted by an eerie silence. All he could hear was his own rapid breathing. He noticed the radio was unplugged as he looked slowly around the room, before his eyes settled on the mess plate Laura had given him earlier. It was sat in the middle of his desk, yet even to his tired, bleary eyes there was something different about it. As he moved closer, he realised what it was. Strangely, inexplicably, there was water in it.

Unsettled and confused, Alan crept to his desk to look more closely at the plate, then jumped back and cried out as he saw a face in the water. It was that of a young man, staring at him with cold, dark eyes. His heart now racing, Alan craned forward, forcing himself to look again. This time he saw nothing other than his own balding, baggy-eyed reflection.

He looked at the plate for a long time, wondering about his state of mind. *Had he really just heard singing from an empty room and seen a face in the water in the mess plate? Was it the drink? But he didn't feel that drunk!*

Standing there bemused, he became aware of a smell,

one he knew well. It was the scent of the sea, a pungent combination of brine and seaweed, so strong that it was as if he were next to a trawler in Stromness. With a palpable shiver, he remembered what Laura had said to him earlier about the plate filling with water and a smell like seaweed.

Eventually, Alan left the room having searched for the source of the smell. After he closed the door, he waited outside for a while, listening for the singing once again, but the study and the house were quiet, save for the ticking of the large hall clock showing quarter to twelve.

Then he looked at the two framed photographs either side of it. One of a tanned, smiling Alison sat in front of the Parthenon on their honeymoon, radiant in a white dress, sunglasses perched on her long, blonde hair. The other picture was of the three of them on a family holiday when Ben was five.

Alan smiled sadly, reflecting on how the grinning boy on the Spanish beach was now a dentist in New Zealand with a wife, Nina, and a son of his own, Oliver. While he yearned to see them, he was glad they couldn't see him at this moment, standing frightened in his hallway, listening outside doors, half sozzled, unsure of what he'd heard and seen.

As Alan's breathing settled, he took a final look at the two photographs, shook his head mournfully, then walked back to the kitchen, where he picked up the bottle of Glenfiddich from the worktop. Without hesitating he poured it down the sink, its tang stinging his nostrils as he did so.

He went back to the lounge, where a rat scurried across the television screen to the accompaniment of a discordant, screeching soundtrack. Alan punched the remote to kill it, then for some reason he couldn't explain, he took a Bible off the bookshelf and went back into the hall to listen for the singing once again, before retiring to bed when he was finally convinced all was quiet.

The Bible remained unopened on the bedside locker, but Alan wanted it there, though he couldn't have explained why. He lay there for a long time, listening, though all he heard was the sighing wind and the distant, ticking clock before he succumbed to a fitful, anxious sleep.

As Remi and Dwight slept over the Atlantic, heads back and open-mouthed, a male steward walked past, then stopped at the row of empty seats to the rear of them. He furrowed his brow at the two wet footprints on the floor of the aircraft directly behind Dwight's seat and wondered what the odd smell was.

8

David Innes arrived at the Scapa Flow Museum at eight thirty a.m., half an hour before the rest of the team showed up, to find Katie already loitering outside by the huge propeller screw of *HMS Hampshire*, her bright auburn tresses whipped by the wind. He smiled and nodded on seeing her and she reciprocated as he approached.

'Great minds, eh,' said David.

'More like safety in numbers. I wasn't prepared to go in on my own, I'll admit.'

'Me neither, if I'm honest,' grinned David as he juggled his big set of keys to find the one for the main door.

He was soon inside and disabling the alarm as Katie hooked their coats up in the main office and switched the lights on.

'Ready?' asked David.

'As I'll ever be,' replied Katie, before taking a deep breath and walking with him into the gallery nearest to the office area, looking about them warily.

'No wet footprints today,' said David as they approached the *Vanguard* display, before his brow creased into a worried frown. Katie gasped at the sight inside the small rectangular cabinet.

It was like an explosion had occurred within; the objects were strewn haphazardly rather than swapped around as they had been the previous evening. The glass was also peppered with star-shaped cracks, as if bullets had been fired from the inside and ricocheted around the cabinet.

'Those objects have hit the glass with some force,' said Katie, running her hand over the damage, where she could feel hairline splits in the surface. At first glance, the items inside didn't appear to be damaged, but they knew they'd need to examine them closely to be sure.

'We'll need to put a notice on it to stop people touching the glass in case they get a cut,' said David.

Katie looked hard at him.

'You're not thinking of opening after this, are you?'

'Well, if the rest of the museum's OK, then why not?'

'Why not? There's some weird activity that's wrecked a display, that's why!' shouted Katie, fear driving her anger. 'If something can smash the glass up like that, how do we know it can't hurt somebody?'

David rubbed his beard, staring at the deranged display.

'But what do I say to the council? What do I say to the staff?' he asked.

'Say what's happened! That's all you can say.'

'I just… it's hard to believe… hard to fathom.'

'That's why we can't open, David. We don't know what we're dealing with here.'

'Aye,' said David with a sigh. 'I'll ring the director and then we'll speak to the staff together. We'll look less mad if we both say it.'

'Then what do we do?' asked Katie.

'Let's see what the director suggests. Maybe a priest or something?'

Katie nodded grimly. Neither had mentioned the two things they were both thinking about – ghosts and hauntings.

Alan Muir stepped outside his front door, grimaced at the dark, scudding clouds and turned up the collar of his coat against the sharp breeze. The mess plate was in a carrier bag at his side as he began the short walk to his kirk, blinking blearily after his disturbed and disturbing night.

Once he'd gone to bed there'd been no more disembodied singing or anything else untoward, not that he'd heard anyway. Yet what had happened deeply unsettled him and he'd been glad to see daylight. There'd not been any more water in the plate when he summoned up the courage to go into the study after breakfast. In fact, everything seemed as it should, leading him to question whether he had really seen and heard such bizarre things the night before. Then he remembered what Laura had said and his experience, certainly in terms of the water in the plate, seemed too similar to be a coincidence. Or was it the result of thought suggestion?

Alan shook his head and pursed his lips, recognising that he was in danger of getting stuck down a rabbit hole. In response, he leant into the wind and strode on more purposefully as the carrier bag flapped by his knee and the plate started to bump annoyingly against his leg.

The electronic ringtone buzzed repeatedly around David Innes's car as he stared at the flashing phone icon on the dashboard while Katie looked out through the rain-streaked windscreen at the shades of grey separating sea from sky. They didn't usually socialise away from work, but both had been shaken by what had occurred and, with an unplanned day off work, Katie was quick to accept David's offer of a coastal drive to the Beneth'ill Café, a place they both liked.

They were returning to Lyness now, filled with coffee and Victoria sponge, and had pulled over on the coast road so David could make his call. Once the answerphone clicked in again, David shook his head and ended the call with an index-fingered stab at the dashboard.

'I can't think where Ally's got to. It's past opening time over there now.'

"Over there" was short-hand for the Stromness Museum on mainland Orkney, which also housed some artefacts from *HMS Vanguard*. David knew Ally Flett, who managed the museum, and had tried contacting him to see if there'd been any issues with his *Vanguard* artefacts. Yet, although it was eleven fifteen a.m. – a quarter of an hour past the Sunday opening time – and David had made two previous calls too, there was still no answer from Ally.

The last two mornings had presented the strangest happenings at the museum in David's six years there. What particularly puzzled him was why these things were happening now. In all the time he'd been there, he'd never seen or heard anything unusual. When he asked Katie if she'd experienced anything strange in her three years as his deputy, she said no too.

They'd been open with the other three staff members when they arrived. They were all equally shocked, particularly when they saw the display. All three also said they'd never encountered anything odd while working there. As a group, they subsequently checked every inch of the museum before closing it. The only issue concerned the *Vanguard* display, hence the call to Ally Flett in Stromness.

The council director had clearly not appreciated a call on a Sunday morning. From the croakiness of his voice, it sounded like he'd been having a lie-in, and his incredulous tone made David feel like a crank. David countered by saying he would send the CCTV footage for the director to view, but the director then fired back with a patronising lecture on how sudden closures could damage tourism and jeopardise jobs, just as David watched Katie at the entrance trying to placate some visitors who had made the trip from mainland Orkney specifically to visit the museum. When David asked what he should do next, the director had said, 'You're the manager. Think of a plan and get back to me tomorrow,' before cutting the call and no doubt putting his head back on his pillow.

Callum Craigie perched forwards on Gary Bremner's sofa, cradling a glass of water that was medicine for his dry throat, though did nothing for his hangover headache or queasy stomach. Gary's loud voice sliced through him from the kitchen, where it seemed to Callum that he was banging cups and bowls down for fun.

'I've told ye before, ye never get anywhere wi' students. They think we're a load o' bumpkin jocks.'

Callum grunted miserably in reply as Gary stuck his head round the door to continue.

'What did Tweddle want wi' you?'

'I'm hoping he can move that plate on for me. I've nae use for it. Might as well take a few quid instead,' replied Callum, swallowing a yawn.

'And it's from the *Vanguard*, ye say? Can I see it?'

'Aye, it's in the back o' ma car,' said Callum, picking up his keys from the coffee table and lobbing them in Gary's direction as he appeared round the door.

As Gary padded down the hall, Callum thought about whether the plate might make him a reasonable amount of money. If it did, giving the other one to Laura might have cost him. Then he reproached himself. He'd given it to her in the hope she'd like it, and if it was worth something, so be it.

Callum counted out the five hundred pounds he owed his friend for the use of the *Peedie Star* and was checking the amount when Gary returned, wrinkling his nose.

'Your car fuckin' stinks, man! Is there a fishin' net in the boot or somethin'?'

'No.'

'Well, it fair stinks. An' the plate doesn't look much, does it?'

'What did ye expect? It's where it's from that's the thing. Anyway, here's your cash for the boat lend. If I don't pay ye now, I'll forget again.'

Gary nodded a thanks and took the money. 'Watch yersel wi' Tweddle. If he tells ye it's worth fifty, it's probably worth a hundred.'

'Aye,' said Callum with a knowing smile.

Alan sat in the front pew of the kirk, hunched over in the cold, looking at the plate on the white altar cloth in front of the large silver cross. Out of habit, he'd lit the candles at each end of the altar and sat absently regarding the left one as his mind churned, trying to make sense of the previous night and what Laura Matson had said to him. He wasn't scared now – daylight and the passing of the hours had scoured the fear away – but he was unsettled, unsure, struggling to understand.

It was so quiet that Alan could hear his own breathing as he closed his eyes, clasped his hands and tried to pray, but it felt hollow, just words in his head going nowhere. As he sat back up, he noticed that the left candle had gone out. So, he looked at the one on the right. The flame suddenly began to sway and flicker before it extinguished abruptly. Alan stood up, looking for the source of the draught, yet there were no open windows. As he did so, his eyes were drawn to the lectern to his right when he heard the urgent rustle and slap of paper. The large Bible's pages had begun to turn over rapidly as if caught in a strong breeze. Alan was transfixed, watching the pages flipping over in a rattling blur. Suddenly, they stopped.

Alan realised he could feel his heart beating and his chest heaved with rapid breaths. He put his hand out in front of him, testing the air for movement. It was still. Then he looked around, even behind him. There was no one there, yet he felt watched as he walked tentatively towards the lectern. The big Bible lay open at Proverbs chapter 3, and he noticed that a small scab of candle wax had somehow travelled at least six feet to land on the margin of the page. Alan read the verse next to the wax out loud.

'Trust in the Lord with all your heart, and do not lean on your own understanding.'

Laura sat at the kitchen table, cradling a coffee mug while reflecting on the brief conversation she'd just had on the phone with Alan Muir. He'd sounded ruffled, very unlike how he'd been when they'd met before, and he was keen to meet as soon as possible.

She didn't know what to make of his cryptic response when she'd asked if everything had been OK with the plate. What did "a few developments for us to discuss" mean? In one sense, she'd hoped nothing untoward had happened to Alan. Yet she was honest enough to admit there was a selfish part of her that hoped something had happened. At least it would prove she wasn't going mad and imagining things. She bit her lip in thought, wondering what would come of their lunchtime meeting later.

9

Remi Binks woke just after seven o' clock at the sound of Kim talking to Holly in the adjacent bedroom, no doubt bouncing her on her knee. He smiled as he heard his daughter giggle and his wife laugh before thinking there'd be more laughter when they opened the gifts he'd bought them in Orkney – a teddy in a kilt for Holly and a Viking-style brooch for Kim.

It was good to be home after his diving holiday, especially after the weirdness of the last two days, which had left him worried for Dwight. He thought about how stressed the guy had looked as they said their goodbyes at JFK, and how obsessed he'd seemed to become over that damn plate. Then there was the thing where he kept fiddling with his finger. All strange, especially for Dwight who had always seemed so sure of himself, so bulletproof.

Remi was pulled from his thoughts into the happy

present as Kim appeared in her pyjamas with a widely smiling Holly on her hip.

'Hi, Daddy!' said Kim as Holly shouted, 'Daddy!' in response.

'Hi, beautiful,' replied Remi, putting his arms out.

'Are those arms for me or her?' asked Kim.

'Both!' laughed Remi.

As Remi was reuniting with his family, David Innes was swinging his Skoda round in the museum car park. It was rainswept and empty, save for Katie's rusting old Fiesta. When he stopped, he rang Ally Flett in Stromness for the fourth time. Again, there was no answer. It was noon. The museum should have been open for an hour.

'I take it you don't have Ally's mobile?'

'If I did, d'ye think I'd still be ringing the museum?' snapped David. He regretted it instantly on seeing Katie's wounded expression. 'I'm sorry, I'm just…'

She nodded understandingly and gave him a conciliatory smile. 'No worries. We're both tense.'

'Aye. It's not every day you close the museum because it's haunted.'

The words were out of his mouth in an unguarded moment. He felt embarrassed and his face flushed. Katie looked into his eyes and nodded again. They both knew what they'd seen and had no other explanation for it.

'What do you plan to do tomorrow?' she asked.

'Get here for eight thirty again and see if anything's happened, then get a contact for Ally through the council.'

'What if his *Vanguard* collection is messed up too?'

'And what if it isn't? Let's just go one step at a time, eh?' said David.

'Well, I'll be here at eight thirty too. Then we're in step together, one at a time, as you say.'

'Thanks Katie,' said David, serious and appreciative. Katie climbed out of the car into the rain.

'Sleep well tonight!' replied Katie with a grin.

'You too!' laughed David thinly.

Alan Muir had made as swift a getaway as was polite after leading the morning service. He turned on his car radio in the hope that it could drown the torrent of thought immediately assailing him now that performing in the kirk was over. Black Sabbath's "Paranoid" boomed out in full, thumping flow.

He swiftly changed stations and "Easy (Like Sunday Morning)" provided a gentler distraction as he climbed out of Kirkwall and headed towards South Ronaldsay. Lunch with Laura awaited – and a predictably strange conversation, given what had happened the previous evening.

Alan was soon thinking about what to say and how to phrase it without sounding a bit unhinged. Laura had just blurted it all out when he met her in town. Had he thought her crazy? Not exactly crazy, but certainly a little odd and highly strung. Now it was his turn to sound odd. He wasn't used to the idea of swapping weird, inexplicable experiences with someone he hardly knew. He was a priest, usually measured and authoritative. At this moment, though, he felt anything but.

Yet there was also a part of him that had become strangely alive. If he could fully believe what he heard and saw last night – the singing and the face in the plate full of water – and the inexplicable indoor breeze this morning, seemingly leading him to a Bible verse, he could surely find his faith again. A belief in God and things beyond his ken, the possibility of an afterlife, the hope that Alison was somewhere else, waiting for him.

As he pondered the idea, he remembered using those worn, woolly phrases with so many bereaved parishioners. "They have passed on and are with God", or "They're now up there, watching over you and waiting". Trite as they were, he'd believed it at the time. Before his own loss had squeezed the faith from him. *Given what had happened with the plate, did it prove there was another dimension? Could he take comfort once again from the idea that people go to a better place?*

Callum huffed in frustration as he braked behind the black Focus in front of him. Fifty on a main road, for God's sake! *Probably an old duffer,* he thought as he edged out to see if it was safe to overtake. It wasn't; a coach with a long line of cars behind it approached in the opposite lane. Callum shouted, 'Shite!' to himself, barely audible above the pounding dance track. Then he pulled a face as the briny smell seemed to become more intense in the car. *Gary was right,* he mused to himself, *the plate or the bag stinks for some reason. Still, it'll be gone soon and hopefully I'll be a few quid better off too.*

Even though he still had the radio on, Alan heard the

urgent note of the red Golf, which had quickly grown in his rear-view mirror and was now so close he couldn't see the end of its bonnet. He smiled to himself, remembering what his driving had been like as a youth; very similar, in fact, to the car now behind him.

As the rain finally stopped, he glanced right at the open waters of Scapa Flow only a farm field away. In many ways it was a stark scene, but also wildly beautiful, capturing in one look how he felt about Orkney; remote and forbidding, yet also homely and comforting.

The last of the procession of cars went past and Callum dropped the Golf into third, accelerating quickly past Alan Muir in a cacophony of howling exhaust and thumping bass. But he didn't disappear into the distance. Callum may have driven fast at times, but he was not crazily reckless. He valued his licence and, while he might go above the limit, it was only where he thought it was safe. The road to St Mary's offered just such a stretch and Callum was now enjoying his journey. As the sky cleared and the sun glittered on Scapa Flow, he swigged a Red Bull and nodded to the beat, oblivious of the wet footprints in the footwell behind him.

Alan gave another indulgent smile as the Golf forged ahead, though he also speeded up to sixty as the road straightened. He started thinking again about his conversation with Laura, the distraction of the flighty Golf and the arresting views having previously snapped his circle of thought.

His new sense of clarity matched the view and he decided to just tell her about his experience in a matter-of-fact way. He wasn't ministering to Laura, after all. They were meeting to discuss what had happened – to both of them, now. If he was somehow vague or indecisive about what had occurred to him it would invalidate what Laura had experienced too. So, he'd just say it and go from there. Wherever "there" was.

Callum had travelled on the road to South Ronaldsay all his life. He knew every bend, side road and undulation, so began to reduce speed as he approached the left-hand bend in the village of St Mary's where the road hugged the shoreline. He braked and dropped down to third in practised style as he began the turn. Suddenly, he felt the steering wheel spin to the right as if immensely strong hands had taken control of his car.

'No!' shouted Callum. The Golf went straight on, then right, careering off the road and bouncing over a small stretch of gravel before rolling over on to the beach in a spray of sand and shingle. As the seatbelt gripped him, Callum was thrown around violently while his fingers dug desperately into the steering wheel. Then his side airbag exploded noisily, buffeting him hard, before the front one smashed into his face in a sulphury-smelling cloud.

Alan was seconds behind and saw the red Golf leave the road and flip, spinning towards the water. As he neared the bend, it had gone out of view, so he pulled sharply to the right, following the route of the Golf, before braking to a halt and jumping out.

The battered car had settled upright in shallow water, facing out to sea. As Alan ran towards it, he grimaced at the heavily dented panels and crazed windows. The glass at the back was missing save for a few jagged pieces around the frame, like fangs in a gaping mouth.

Alan was soon splashing alongside the car, almost too frightened to look at what he might see inside. When he did look through the cracked side window, he saw the white billowing airbags and the outline of a head. Fortunately, the water was lapping just below the door so opened without resistance, releasing a smell like burnt rubber.

'Hello, son! Can you hear me?' asked Alan, his tone urgent.

Callum was silent, his face a sickening mask of red. Alan forced himself to look more closely and saw the lad's nose was split lengthways, probably from the airbag, he thought. He pushed the side airbag down and felt for a pulse in his neck, sighing with relief when he found it and on seeing the slight rise of his chest.

There was a shout from behind him and the sound of running feet grinding on the beach, then splashing in the water as a big, bearded man in overalls and a flat cap loomed up beside him.

'I've rung 999. I've asked for all three services.'

'Sorry?'

'Fire, ambulance and police.'

'Right,' said Alan, feeling stupid. 'He's breathing, but he's unconscious and his face is a mess.'

'It could go on fire here,' said the man.

'But it's in water.'

'Aye, seawater, which won't mix well wi' battery acid.'

'Oh, OK. But you're told not to move a casualty, aren't you?'

'In that case, I'll keep a close eye on the bonnet while you watch him.'

Alan nodded and pressed a tissue to Callum's nose. As they waited anxiously for the emergency services, Alan glanced around the car. A shiver passed through him as he saw a mess plate, identical to the one Laura had given him, sat neatly in the front passenger footwell, as if it had been placed there when the car stopped rolling. It was completely intact.

10

Jean Craigie sat at her son Callum's hospital bedside, holding his hand. He was dozing, propped up in a blue hospital gown under white covers. A livid red scar closed by several stitches ran down much of his nose. Thankfully, Callum had regained consciousness within a few minutes of the crash and was in a bed in Balfour Hospital within the hour.

Jean had spoken to him briefly, but he was confused owing to concussion and the doctor had advised her just to let him rest. She'd cried on seeing Callum's battered car on the shore at St Mary's as they rushed to the hospital. As Shona had been driving, Jean couldn't help but look at the frightening sight. It was such a relief to see Callum alive and in one piece on arrival.

The doctors had said there were no bones broken, though his face would bruise up from the airbag and he would be stiff and sore. The hospital's main concern was that he'd been knocked out and clearly had concussion. He therefore needed to stay in hospital for at least a couple of days for regular observation.

Shona sat the opposite side of Callum's bed to Jean. She looked at her nephew with a concerned frown and shook her head slightly.

'Penny for them,' said Jean.

Shona looked at her sister and took a while to reply.

'Now's not the time,' she said softly, looking back at Callum.

Jean nodded, adding, 'Later, though?'

'Aye,' said Shona, pleased her sister wanted to hear her opinion and hopefully her advice.

'Lemon cake?' asked Laura Matson.

'Oh yes, lovely,' replied Alan Muir. He was sitting at Laura's kitchen table. His stopping at Callum's crash had put paid to their lunch at Robertson's Coffee Hoose and there were no tables available for a later slot, though Alan was more than content with a ham sandwich and some cake at Laura's house, given that it was now mid-afternoon.

He was just starting to relax a little after the heart-thumping fear he'd felt earlier in St Mary's. Though it had been a moment of huge relief when Callum regained consciousness, witnessing the accident had been a shock. It also knocked the scab off an old and very deep wound. Alan had not been present when Alison had died on the road, but every time he saw an accident, even on the television or in a newspaper, it was a painful trigger. To see Callum looking lifeless through the cracked car window was not something he could easily put to the back of his mind.

The bottoms of his trousers were finally starting to dry and his socks lay over a radiator at Laura's insistence. So far, they'd just talked about the crash. Laura had been shocked to find out it had been Callum, who'd told Alan his name when he came round. Meanwhile, the plate from Callum's Golf was now in the boot of Alan's car. He intended to tell Laura about it to see if she knew anything more.

Once they were tucking into their cake, full tea mugs at their elbows, Laura dived in.

'So, what's happened? These "developments" you talked about?' she asked.

'When exactly?'

'Well, last night for a start.'

Alan swallowed a bite of cake, paused while finding the words, then began.

'Strange things happened last night, like they did to you. Things I've never experienced before and can't explain; so bizarre, in fact, I've wondered if they were real. Truth be told, I'd had a few drams and even asked myself if it was that, but I wasn't really… intoxicated.'

Laura nodded and smiled encouragingly at Alan. It confirmed her experience wasn't imagined, for a start.

'What did you see?' she asked.

'Well, first of all, it wasn't what I *saw*, it was what I *heard*. There was singing, male voices singing "Heart of Oak", an old naval song. It wasn't like a choir; more like a group of men just having a singsong, like at a rugby club. I thought it was some drunks outside at first, but then I realised it was inside, in the study.'

'Where was the plate?'

'In the study! Then when I went in, the singing stopped. I checked the radio – definitely switched off. I looked all round but couldn't find anywhere the singing could've come from. Then I noticed the plate had water in it and, when I looked closer, I saw a face in it. It definitely wasn't my reflection.'

Laura was quiet as she absorbed what Alan had said.

'Was there any smell?'

'Oh, aye. Yes, like a briny smell, but it wasn't there this morning.'

'I had the smell too, remember. But nothing happened here last night. It looks like the plate's the issue.'

Alan nodded. 'Aye, it does.'

'Where's the plate now?' asked Laura.

'On the altar in my church. I took it down early before the service this morning. That brings me to weird experience number two.'

'Go on,' said Laura, before eating her final mouthful of cake.

'I took the plate to the church, thinking that putting it in a consecrated environment might somehow help. So, I placed it on the altar and the candles blew out, yet there was no draught, no windows or doors open, nothing. Then the pages in the Bible on the lectern started flicking over as if they were caught in a wind. After the pages stopped turning, I went to the Bible and there was a spot of candle wax on the page next to a particular verse, which was, “Trust in the Lord with all your heart, and do not lean on your own understanding.”’

‘Couldn’t that just be coincidence? The wax landing on the Bible?’

‘If it was, the wax had jumped about six feet! I’ve never seen that before, and I’ve been a priest a long time,’ said Alan with a weak smile.

Laura was quiet again, serious-faced, mulling it all over as she held her mug in both hands.

‘Then there was mystery number three,’ he added. Laura’s eyes widened. ‘When Callum went off the road and I opened the door, there was another plate, identical to the one you passed to me, in the front of his car.’

‘I remember now. He’d said there was one for each of us when he gave it me.’

‘But the really strange thing is, it was intact,’ said Alan.

‘I don’t follow.’

‘The car rolled several times, Laura. It was really smashed up. When I looked inside, things had been thrown all over – drinks cans, spilled mints. Yet the plate sat on the floor mat on the passenger side like it’d been glued there.’

‘Where is it now?’

‘In the boot of my car. I’m going to put it in the church with the other one.’

‘This gets more and more scary, Alan.’

‘And confusing. While Callum was in no state to say why he might’ve crashed, there’s no obvious explanation. He overtook me but I wouldn’t say he was going so fast that he could have spun off the road. It made me think twice about putting the plate in my car,' he replied grimly.

'Yet we've both driven with the other plate in our cars and been OK. Doesn't that suggest it's not the plate that caused him to crash?'

'Who knows?' said Alan with a sigh.

They finished their tea in quiet reflection, then Laura asked another question.

'So, what next?'

'I'm going to contact my bishop for advice. This stuff is way beyond me.'

'When?'

'As soon as I'm home. I'll ring you as soon as I know something concrete.'

'Thanks,' said Laura. 'Let's hope for a quiet night.'

'I'll be praying for one,' said Alan, suddenly aware he meant it.

Jean wrinkled her nose as her sister, Shona, bustled through the hospital exit ahead of her and lit a cigarette. Like many former smokers, Jean now hated the smell of tobacco with the passion of a religious convert. She stood a short distance away and faced Shona, who sucked her cheeks in and took a long drag.

'I've an idea what you're goin' t' say, Shona.'

'Go on,' said Shona as she exhaled.

'Ye think Callum's accident was something t' do with that plate.'

Shona gave a small nod.

'How does that work?' asked Jean.

'God only knows! I just feel it, Jean. Neither the police nor Callum could explain why he went off the road.'

'The police just said they couldn't explain it *for now* and would be examining the car further. And as for Callum, he doesn't know what bloody day it is at the moment.'

'I feel it, Jean! I feel strongly that Callum having that plate is all wrong, and you know I've been right on these things before.'

Jean couldn't deny that Shona had some kind of power that couldn't be explained. She also knew her older sister was honest and would want the best for her and Callum.

'What's to be done then?' asked Jean.

Shona shook her head. 'I don't know. Really, I don't. But I reckon the key to this is where the plate came from. If Callum knows that, it might point the way.'

'He told us he didn't know – and you heard the doctor, he's to be left to rest.'

'Aye, I know, but maybe tomorrow he'll be up to some gentle questioning. We still don't know why Callum crashed!' said Shona, pulling urgently on her cigarette.

II

Laura took her white wine from The Murray Arms' bar and headed for the bench seat under the window; the side tables and stools were already occupied. No sooner had she sat down than Shona Drever walked in.

'I'll have a large merlot please, Tina. I need it!' declared Shona.

On receiving her wine, Shona spotted the empty space next to Laura and headed for it. They were on nodding terms, but didn't really know each other, though Laura was glad for any company if it distracted her from thoughts of the plates.

'It's Laura, isn't it?'

'It is, though I'm sorry, I, er...'

'I'm Shona.'

Laura raised her glass in acknowledgement and Shona clinked hers against it.

'Cheers,' announced Shona, before taking a big gulp.

'Cheers,' replied Laura, taking a sip.

'I know you're friendly with Callum, my nephew,' said Shona, her face suddenly serious.

'How is he? I heard about the accident.'

'News travels fast as always on Orkney, eh. He's concussed, has a nasty cut on his nose and has been generally bashed about as the car's flipped over, but he's still in one piece,' said Shona with a tight smile.

'I was talking to the guy who was first on the scene earlier. He said it was a bad crash, with Callum's car ending up in the shallows.'

'Aye, another few yards into the water and he could've drowned.'

There was a pause as Shona started to make the connection.

'So, you know Alan Muir, the priest from Kirkwall?' asked Shona.

'A little bit,' said Laura.

'D'you go to his kirk then?'

'No, I'm not a churchgoer. I, er, only met him the other day. It was here actually, y'know when that American shouted at you outside and Alan stepped in?'

'Oh, aye. It was Alan who talked him round. Mind you, that Yank's heading for trouble. He wasn't for listening though,' said Shona with a wry look.

'What do you mean?'

'Well, I see spirits sometimes and on Friday I saw one behind him. Just over there, in fact,' said Shona, nodding towards the corner of the bar where Dwight had been standing with Remi and Callum.

'You see spirits? Like ghosts?' asked Laura, intrigued, yet also a little unnerved at this bizarre turn in the conversation.

'Aye, I do, whether you believe it or not,' said Shona with a direct look.

'Two days ago, I wouldn't have believed you, but now I think there's definitely something in it,' replied Laura with a nervous laugh.

'Why d'you say that?'

Laura took a sip of wine, checked to see if others in the bar seemed to be listening, then recounted what had happened to her on the Friday night, followed by what Alan Muir had told her earlier. She described every bizarre experience, the sounds, sights and smells. While she wasn't sure she should have said anything about Alan, Shona had the sort of gaze that seemed to be able to look into you. As a result, Laura found herself telling her all of it.

Shona listened intently, largely impassive as she absorbed the information, save for the occasional confirmatory nod, almost as if it was what she expected to hear. After a pause and another slug of wine, Shona spoke quietly.

'I knew it was all down to the plates,' she said. 'When the Yank passed them to Callum, that's when I saw the sailor behind him. Then when I saw the plate on the hall table at Jean's, it had an aura, like a brooding presence.'

'I find all this weird and pretty frightening, to be honest,' said Laura. Shona nodded sympathetically.

'What's worrying with this is Callum's crash. If that's somehow linked to the plates, we're in dangerous waters,' replied Shona. 'Did Callum tell you where the plates were from?'

'No, but I presume those Americans found them on a dive. I saw they'd been out on a boat with Callum earlier that day. They moored near the ferry terminal on the small jetty on Pier Road.'

'Really! Now, I didn't know that. Looks like they've been poking around underwater where they shouldn't have, somehow.'

'Has Callum been asked where the plates are from?' asked Laura.

'Not with him being concussed, no,' said Shona, draining her glass. 'How about another?'

'OK, but I'm paying,' said Laura, brandishing a twenty-pound note.

After a jittery but otherwise uneventful homeward journey with the plate in the boot, Alan Muir had taken it to the kirk and placed it on the altar next to the other one. Save for a little yellowing on the edge of the plate Laura had passed to him, they were identical. He'd handled Callum's plate from the car almost as if it was a bomb, yet once he was in the church and there was no evidence of any disturbance, he relaxed a little before saying the Lord's prayer aloud. The line "deliver us from evil" had never been more heartfelt.

Once he was home, Alan rang his bishop's secretary, who quickly found the number he should call. It was for a priest in Carlisle called Helen Hughes, who answered on the fourth ring in a clear, pleasant Welsh accent.

'Hello, Helen Hughes.'

'Oh, hello. My name's Alan Muir. I'm an Episcopalian priest in Orkney and I've been given your details by my diocese.'

'Good evening.'

'Good evening to you too. Sorry to bother you on a Sunday, but it's something important I'd like some advice on.'

'Well, can you tell me a little more? Oh, just hold on; let me get settled in the chair.'

Alan heard some muffled movement and the mewing of a cat at the other end of the phone.

'Right, OK. The cat's nicely settled on my lap now, so talk away,' said Helen.

'I've experienced some goings-on that I can't explain. Me and a young woman, and possibly a young man who is in hospital after a car crash today.'

'Oh dear. Is he badly injured?'

'Thankfully, no. Concussion and cuts and bruises. I actually reached the car first after it left the road,' said Alan, a jolt of adrenaline surging through him as he recalled the accident.

'My goodness! So, what exactly has been going on?'

Alan described what had happened to Laura and to him over the last few days in relation to the plate and its seemingly indestructible twin he had found in Callum's car. He wasn't one to naturally over-share, though he found this woman easy to speak to.

'I have to say, Helen, this thing's knocked me sideways. I've never seen or heard anything like this and I'll be honest, I've questioned my sanity. It's only the fact that there's someone else saying similar things that makes me believe it's real.'

'Clearly something strange is going on, Alan. Can you please email me everything you've just told me so I can share it with our team?'

'Yes, no problem. Do you think you'll be able to travel up to us?' asked Alan.

Helen gave a politician's answer.

'That'll be up to the bishop, who'll take his steer from the team. I hope I can help though, so email me as soon as possible and I'll get back to you.'

'OK, I'll get on with it now. Thanks, Helen.'

Once they had swapped email addresses and landline back-up numbers and said goodbye, both sat back and reflected on the call. Helen stroked Colin's ginger fur absent-mindedly, wondering what the probability of two people having the same hallucinations were, particularly when they were in separate locations and, from the sounds of it, not that familiar with each other. Alan also seemed perfectly rational and had the usual doubts and fears that supernatural phenomena evoked.

Meanwhile, Alan wondered whether he had sounded sane and shaken rather than unhinged and linked to a similarly unbalanced younger sidekick.

It was just after eight p.m. when Alan levered himself off the sofa and padded into the kitchen seeking sustenance. A packet of crisps on the worktop seemed to beckon to him. They were something he always enjoyed with a cold lager, but as he reached the fridge, he checked himself, brought out the milk instead and made a cup of tea. The crisps were also ignored as Alan sought alternative comfort from a handful of digestives that would soon be dunked in the tea as he watched the football highlights. For a short while at least, the bizarre happenings and Callum Craigie's accident were parked while Alan focused on his beloved Hearts FC.

12

Dwight O'Neil sat back and looked around the huge oval of the MetLife Stadium with a satisfied smile, his old, faded green Jets cap shading his eyes. He'd had a top-tier season ticket that looked down directly on the fifty-yard line for a decade and had only missed three games in those ten years. His father had been an avid Jets fan and ensured that both his sons followed suit.

Yet Dwight wasn't the average fan. In his youth he had excelled at football. He'd been a star quarterback in High School and went on to represent Princeton with such distinction that a pro football career seemed likely, until his throwing arm was mangled in a grudge match against Yale. Surgery and rehabilitation enabled him to play again, but the extra length and snap of his passing were lost, and with it, his glittering gridiron dreams.

Failure and disappointment were uncommon feelings for Dwight, so he decided that if he couldn't play pro, he wouldn't play at all. While he hadn't thrown a ball in anger since his college days, Dwight still loved the game and studied it with the academic scrutiny typical of a former quarterback who used to dictate the play. It meant that the regulars who sat around him at the games had to suffer a loud non-stop commentary, though at least it was well-informed.

'Nothing like it when it's full, huh, Dwight?' said Joe Holland, who sat to his left in his regulation Jets jersey stretched over a sizeable girth. Heavy-set, bearded and foul-mouthed, Joe provided a passionate accompaniment to proceedings that compensated in volume for what it lacked in insight. Dwight smiled and nodded as he savoured the spectacle and the sound.

To Dwight's right, Carlos and Gloria Marquez were in some ways the opposite of Joe. Both were slight and quiet, and always philosophically stoic when the Jets lost. It was a different matter when the Jets scored, however. They would then both explode in frenzied animation. In fact, Gloria had kissed Dwight in elation many times following a touchdown and, when she'd occasionally swapped seats with her husband, so had Carlos.

Directly in front of Dwight sat Vinnie. Dwight didn't know his second name, and most of the fans in the section only knew him by his nickname of BS, the abbreviation of "bullshit", which he shouted with irritating frequency whenever a decision went against the Jets.

There were also many other familiar faces around him.

Faces he'd seen expressing the full range of human emotion in response to the unpredictable nature of sport that made it so enthralling, particularly when you identified with one of its tribes, as Dwight did with the Jets.

Dwight was invariably happy in his lofty perch at the imposing MetLife Stadium. The people around him were like a second family, and in many ways more agreeable than his real one. They certainly disagreed with him less than his brother seemed to and didn't keep asking him why he wasn't married like his mother did. And for the time being, Dwight's recent travails were largely forgotten.

After the drive home from the airport, Dwight had left his bags in the Hummer in the secure car park beneath his apartment block and poured a very large Jack Daniels, which delivered a quick knockout blow. It meant that he'd slept for seven hours until waking with a sore head and dry mouth. Thankfully, it had been a drunk, dreamless sleep, and though he'd padded groggily to the bathroom on waking, the ragged edge of nerves he'd recently felt had thankfully gone, though his finger was still dead for some reason.

While he was tired from the flights, still shaken from yesterday's panic attack and a little befuddled by recent experiences, Dwight's Sunday had passed uneventfully and at times proved quite enjoyable. Indeed, a leisurely lunch with his cousin Michael at a waterfront restaurant, a long pier-side walk in glorious September sunshine and the anticipation of the evening game had all proved healthy distractions that reduced the heat from his simmering worries.

Consequently, as the Jets and the Patriots flooded on to the pitch amid raucous cheering, Dwight was simply in the moment, raising his voice with the green clad throng around him.

'J-E-T-S, Jets! Jets! Jets!'

Dwight was soon engrossed in what was to be a close and thrilling game. The Patriots quietened the home crowd with a touchdown five minutes into the first quarter, then a field goal at the start of the second. It was virtually silent apart from some angry shouts directed at the officials, and a few at some unfortunate players identified as at fault by raucous fans.

'Bullshit!' roared Vinnie as the referee penalised a Jets player for encroachment.

An equally loud, 'Jerk!' was barked by Joe next to Dwight's ear, causing him to wince. Dwight stayed quiet, having spotted the Jets' defensive linesman move early and clearly into an offside position. The officials may have been right, but at ten points to nil, it seemed that somebody had to be on the receiving end of the home fans' frustration.

By half-time though, the Jets' fans were in a different mood as their team went into the break 14-10 in front, following two touchdowns of their own. Both clever passing moves had Dwight purring with appreciation.

'It'll be interesting to see if they keep looking to pass or mix it up with a few runs,' said Dwight to Gloria as they waited for the start of the third quarter. Gloria had some binoculars and offered them to Dwight.

'Have a look-see at the bench, spot who might be getting ready,' she said, passing them across.

Dwight nodded his thanks, aimed the binoculars at the bench area and scrolled his left finger on the focusing wheel between the eye pieces, his right still numb and useless. He was soon identifying who was standing and helmeted, ready to play, and who was sat down still, waiting for involvement. As he did so, in the proliferation of green and white uniforms, he noticed some dark blue on the second bench. He locked on to the figure and his eyes widened.

In the second row of players was a sailor in navy-blue uniform. He was young, slight, bare-headed, with short, dark hair. As Dwight refocused, having wavered with the binoculars in shock, the sailor seemed to look up, as if staring directly at him. His eyes were hard, angry, accusing. Dwight dropped the glasses down for a moment before he looked back through the binoculars to make sure the sailor was really there. He quickly found him again and as he settled his focused gaze, the sailor looked up again with the same stony face.

'What's up, Dwight? You look like you've seen a ghost,' said Gloria, noticing the shock on his face.

'Just take a look at the bench, Gloria. See anything unusual?' asked Dwight as he passed the binoculars back to her, trying to sound casual as his stomach seemed to knot.

Gloria scanned the bench area for a while then lowered the binoculars.

'What exactly am I looking for? I can just see the players and staff milling around.'

'Can you see a sailor?'

'A sailor!' exclaimed Gloria.

'Yeah, I… er… thought I saw one in the second row. Must be like a veteran invited on to the bench or somethin.'

It sounded odd, even to Dwight. Gloria looked again.

'Second row, you say? I can't see any sailor, Dwight.' She looked at him, puzzled.

Dwight put his hand out for the binoculars.

'Let's see if he's still there,' said Dwight.

When he looked this time, there was no sailor there.

The last two quarters were as thrilling as the first two; the Patriots stealing the win with the last play of the game 38-34. Yet Dwight sat silent and impassive, the on-field drama not really registering, as if his eyes were open but he couldn't see. As Vinnie and Joe kept up their verbal barrage, Gloria took a few sideways glances at Dwight. She'd never seen him so quiet, nor notice him continually flexing his right hand before.

13

As he sat at the stern of the *Peedie Star* in a gentle swell facing a grinning Dwight, Remi couldn't believe he was back on Scapa Flow, heading towards the marker buoy for *HMS Vanguard* once again. His anger at Dwight's antics the year before had dissipated with time and, while he felt conflicted about returning to the *Vanguard*, Dwight's offer to pay for his trip out of the seventy thousand dollars he'd made selling the mess plate had been enough to finally persuade Remi to go. The sky was blue, the weather mild and the breeze benign. It was perfect for diving, yet Remi was wrestling internally, just as he had twelve months ago.

As for Dwight, he looked as happy as could be and certainly different than he had in the days after the dive last year, when he'd seemed to have some sort of meltdown. His fixation with the plate had come good too when he'd found a private collector willing to pay well for it. *It's typical Dwight O'Neil,* thought Remi.

'You got your shopping bag?' laughed Dwight as Remi gave him a desultory nod and held up his black dive sack before he looped it over his shoulder, his doubts over the venture growing seemingly by the second.

'Just think of all those plates waiting for us, Remi! The ship's like a fuckin' gold mine.'

'We don't know that, Dwight. It blew up, remember. The ones you found last time might be the only ones intact,' replied Remi wearily.

They'd discussed the chances of finding more plates repeatedly. Dwight insisted there'd be more because the ship had such a big crew and therefore hundreds of plates, while Remi maintained that the destruction of the ship would mean that few survived the blast and any that did would be difficult to find on three time-limited dives, which was all Callum would agree to, even for ten thousand pounds. As usual, though, Dwight's money talked and here they were again, even if Remi felt uncomfortable.

The yellow and black buoy swayed lazily on the rippling surface as Remi and Dwight confirmed the timings with Callum before stepping off the boat. Saltwater stung Remi's eyes as they resurfaced to don their masks, synchronise dive computers and give each other the customary thumbs-down that signalled their return to *HMS Vanguard*.

The year before, they'd found its remains almost immediately. They were just as fortunate this time. Within seconds of levelling out at fifty feet, their lights played over the bow section rising tall from the seabed. To Remi, the impact of seeing the *Vanguard* again was no less thrilling than the first time. If anything, he felt even sadder. And, given the purpose of the dive, he also felt something else: shame.

Remi was soon following Dwight down towards the port-side of the bow. The wreckage grew in their torch beams until they were only six feet away from its towering form. They went lower, stopping when suspended just above the sea floor, where the metal plates of the hull had buckled outwards, exposing the inside of the officers' quarters. Remi played his torch inside the gap in the hull, picking out some rusty bedframes lying on jagged teak planking. It was as much as he wanted to see and he retreated from the ship as Dwight swam forwards and began reaching inside. Remi had no heart for this and simply marked time, watching the back of Dwight's black hooded head sporadically wreathed in bursts of bubbles as he probed inside the wreck.

Suddenly, Dwight jerked forwards as if pulled from within. He seemed to be wrestling to stay outside and braced his left leg against the crumpled outer plate. Remi swam to his aid, illuminating the gap. Bile rose into Remi's throat in fear at what he saw. A brawny, tattooed arm had grasped Dwight's right hand and seemed to be dragging him into the darkness of the wreck.

Remi reached in to try to free the hand, only to be grabbed by another. As he struggled desperately to free himself, he caught a glimpse of the tattoo on the forearm in his falling torch beam. It read "vengeance".

'Remi, Remi, you're OK,' said Kim soothingly as Remi woke. He was lathered in sweat, panting in short gasps, and his chest heaved as he came to, realising it had been a nightmare. As his breathing slowed and he started to calm down, he levered himself up and sat on the edge of the bed before fumbling for the side light.

Kim touched his bare, clammy back concernedly.

'Baby, you're soaked through.'

'I had a nightmare,' croaked Remi.

'That's rare. I'm the one that has the bad dreams. What was it about?'

'Diving, and I… er… got trapped.'

'I can't remember you dreaming about diving before,' said Kim.

'I dream about it a lot, but it's usually pleasant,' replied Remi, rising to go to the bathroom.

Remi splashed cold water on his face and stared through puffy eyes at his reflection in the mirror. He looked as bad as he felt, though his equilibrium was returning as the realisation it had been a dream sank in.

Then he remembered how Dwight had cried out in his sleep when they'd been on Orkney the day they'd dived to the *Vanguard*. He also recalled how Dwight had looked just before they went their separate ways at JFK. He'd been haggard and anxious. As his diving partner's face came into his mind's eye, Remi's concern for Dwight panged. As he padded back to bed and smiled at Kim, laying on her side watching him return, he resolved to text Dwight in the morning.

David Innes pulled up opposite the only other car in the museum car park, which was Katie's ageing Fiesta. He was quickly out into the fresh morning breeze and savouring the open sky as Katie crossed the concourse.

'Morning, boss!' chirped Katie.

'Morning, pleb!' retorted David with a grin. He hated to be called "boss" and she knew it.

It was false cheerfulness, at odds with their churning stomachs and dry mouths, as they approached the entrance door. David quickly found the correct key and, after a deep breath and tight smile at Katie, opened up and walked in as warily as he had the day before. He quickly entered his office, silenced the alarm, punched the "on" button on his desk computer to warm it up, and looked around to check all was as it had been left the day before. So far, it was.

'All OK?' asked Katie.

'Aye, in here at least. Ready for a wander round?'

'Of course. I've got my cross and holy water,' said Katie with a smile.

'It's no laughing matter,' replied David, his face serious.

'I know. I'm just trying to brave it out, y'know.'

'Aye. I know.'

They approached the *Vanguard* display case in circumspect fashion once again, though they could see no change from the day before. Katie had photographed it using her phone and she was soon comparing the picture with the case as they saw it today.

'Looks the same to me,' said Katie.

'Aye, it does. No footprints either. Come on, let's check the rest of the site.'

To their relief, the museum was as it had been left the previous day and there were no wet footprints anywhere, so they returned to the office, where David made them a coffee while Katie looked online to find a glazier who could repair the *Vanguard* display case.

'Are we opening, then?' she asked.

'Aye, I think we do. There's no sign of anything wrong, so let's ring the staff and get them in.'

Katie nodded. She remained unsettled but could see that David would come under fire from the council director if he didn't open the museum after a night without anything untoward happening – at least that they could detect.

'I'll look at the CCTV from last night though, just to see if anything comes up. Oh, and I'll ring Ally Flett again over in Stromness to see if anything's happened there.'

'What about the *Vanguard* display?'

'I've thought about that. We cover the whole thing with a tarpaulin and put a sign on – y'know, "display temporarily unavailable" or somethin' like that. We've got those green tarps in the store,' said David.

'Are we taking the artefacts out of the case first?'

'Do you want to do it?'

'No way!' laughed Katie nervously.

'Me neither!' said David with a grin. 'We'll just cover the bloody thing.'

The next twenty minutes were busy. Katie booked the glazier, rang the staff and changed the website information to show they were open, while David braved the storeroom on his own, located the green tarpaulin and covered the *Vanguard* display with it, before sticking a notice on it, simply stating:

DISPLAY AWAITING REFURBISHMENT

As Katie greeted the arriving staff and prepared to open up to the public, David started working through the CCTV, emailed the council director to say they were opening and rang the council offices at nine a.m. to see if they would provide him with Ally Flett's mobile number. Frustratingly, they wouldn't, on the grounds of "not being at liberty to release personal information", despite David's pleading that it was an important work matter. So, as Katie greeted an elderly couple at the museum desk at nine thirty a.m., David carried on looking at CCTV footage. While it was monotonous watching a film where nothing happened, to David, the lack of any activity was also something of a relief.

It was a sunny morning in Kirkwall and Alan Muir was savouring a takeout cappuccino on a bench outside St Magnus's Cathedral when his mobile rang.

'Hello, Alan Muir.'

'Morning, Alan. It's Helen Hughes.'

'Oh, hello there,' said Alan, placing his beaker next to him on the bench and wiping a thin moustache of milky foam from his upper lip.

'I'm ringing to say that I've had the go-ahead to travel to Orkney, got my cat-sitter at short notice and can come tomorrow if that's OK?'

'Oh, that'd be great.'

'Well, I'm hoping to book on the Glasgow flight that'll

get me to Kirkwall for ten thirty in the morning. Would it be possible for you to pick me up?'

'Of course. Where do you intend to stay?' asked Alan.

'I hadn't thought that far yet. I was getting the flight sorted out first.'

'Well, you're welcome to stay with me. I've a spare room.'

'Oh, thank you. That sounds fine and the bishop will be pleased – it'll keep the expenses down.'

They chuckled in unison before saying their goodbyes. The smile stayed on Alan's face as he reached for his coffee. He was more relaxed as he'd had no issues the previous evening and Laura had also texted to happily report another uneventful night. Then his phone pinged, alerting him to a text from Helen Hughes.

It said:

> P.S. I read your email. Disturbing stuff! Was all OK last night? Best wishes, Helen.

Alan smiled again, thought carefully about his reply, then texted:

> Hi Helen. All OK last night at both mine and Laura's. I'll check the kirk later and let you know. Look forward to meeting you tomorrow. Best wishes, Alan.

Shona spotted Jean walking Lady, the family collie, on Pier Road as she came out of the general store with her morning paper. She waved to her sister and Jean put her hand up in turn to acknowledge she'd seen her. Lady pulled hard, tongue lolling and tail wagging, striving to get to Shona as quickly as she could.

'Hiya,' said Shona. 'Grand morning!'

'Aye, it is. Lady's pulled me all round St Margaret's Hope!'

'I'll bet,' said Shona as she bent to fuss her, receiving a slobbery hand from Lady's energetic licking.

'I'm away to see Callum shortly,' said Jean.

'How is he?'

'Doing alright. I rang the Balfour earlier and they said he'd had a good night, was a lot brighter and they may let him home tomorrow if all's well.'

'That's great. It'll be good for you to get him back home.'

'Too true! I rang him before I came out and he sounded more himself. He'd had a breakfast as well, which was good.'

'If he's thinking about his stomach again, it's a good sign,' said Shona with a smile.

'Aye, he likes his food right enough. He wants me to take him some chocolate biscuits in!'

'And why not?' laughed Shona. 'I'll pop to the shop if ye like and get some. I'd like to see him too, if that's OK.'

There was a pause as Jean looked down, as if trying to find the right words, before looking at Shona, her eyes serious.

'Can you leave it today, Shona, and let me go on my own,' said Jean. It was more a statement than a question.

'Well, I would like to see Callum. I—'

'You mean you'd like to wheedle at him to find out more about these bloody plates?' snapped Jean.

Silence ensued. Lady sensed the tension and sat down with her ears flat, searching the faces of both sisters.

'Your son nearly died yesterday and you're in denial about what's going on!' said Shona sharply.

'And what exactly is going on Shona, eh? Please tell me!' said Jean, her voice rising. 'All we know is that my lad's in the hospital and you're blethering on about ghosts and plates. Same old Shona. Ye've got to be at the centre of everything!'

Shona looked pained but said no more. She simply turned around and walked away, heading for home.

David Innes's eyes were tiring after half an hour staring at CCTV images recorded near the *Vanguard* display. It was just a monotonous, monochrome scene of nothing happening whatsoever. As he sat back, stretched and yawned loudly, he realised it had turned ten a.m. and the museum in Stromness should be open.

He dialled the number and after a few seconds of purring, a loud, thick Glaswegian brogue cut in.

'Hello!'

'Is that Ally? It's David Innes from Scapa Flow Museum.'

'Hello, David! Aye, it's me, the one and only!' said Ally jocularly. 'What can I do you for?'

'Is everything OK there? I tried ringing yesterday and there was no answer.'

'Aye, well, we were closed over the weekend. I had a stomach bug and Julie was off wi' it too. Must've been the take-oot sandwiches we had on Friday. Julie's still off today, though I'm a bit more solid, if ye get ma meaning.'

'Sorry t'hear that, but is everything OK with the museum?' asked David, twiddling a pencil.

'I think so. To be honest, I've only just got in and opened up. Why d'ye ask?'

'It's just that we've had some unexplained happenings here.'

'Like what?' Ally sounded intrigued.

'Well. The artefacts in our *Vanguard* display were all messed up when we came in on Saturday morning and we don't know how. I wondered if anything weird had happened at your spot?'

'Well, I can go and look. I'll get back to ye, OK?'

'Righto, Ally,' said David, suddenly feeling silly having spoken aloud about what had happened.

Within five minutes, David's phone rang. It was Ally.

'The *Vanguard* stuff is all mixed up! It's fuckin' amazin! And that's what's happened over wi' you as well?' asked Ally excitedly.

'Two nights running, aye. Is there any damage or anything else strange?'

'No damage, just like someone's got in the display case and decided to swap stuff about. Looks like we've a ghost moving between the museums. The restless spirit of a sailor stalking our corridors, eh!'

'It's not funny, Ally. It's freaked us out here. We've had wet footprints on Friday night too, picked up on CCTV.'

'Awesome! Can you send me the images? I'd love t'see that!' enthused Ally.

'Aren't you worried?' asked David.

'Not really. I've done a bit o' ghost hunting in the past. Seen and heard all sorts o' crazy shit over the years. Apparitions, voices, orbs, flying objects… the lot!'

David didn't know what orbs were and didn't have the inclination to ask. He just wanted things back to normal.

'What d'you suggest we do?' asked David.

'If you're worried about it, and it sounds like ye are, I'd get a medium in to see if they can work out what's happening,' said Ally.

'How do I go about finding a medium?'

'Oh, that's nae bother. I know one. Shona Drever down in St Margaret's Hope on South Ronaldsay. She made contact with my grandad for me. A nice woman.'

David's eyebrows arched in surprise. The whole thing became ever more bizarre.

'Do you have her number?'

'Oh aye, just gimme a sec,' said Ally.

14

Laura was enjoying a brisk afternoon walk after a lazy morning phone-scrolling and reading the Sunday paper, before a hefty bacon sandwich had left her feeling stodgy and in need of some exercise. After another uneventful night, she was more relaxed. She was looking at the horizon in a gap between the houses, contemplating bringing her easel and paints down to the shore, when her phone rang, the shrill bell-like tone cutting through the quietness. She stopped and took the phone out, noting the call was from Alan Muir.

'Hi, Alan,' said Laura, slightly breathless.

'Hi, Laura. Are you OK to talk?'

'Yeah. I'm just having a walk, getting a bit of air, actually.'

'Making the most of the fine weather, eh?'

'Something like that,' said Laura. 'Any news on the deliverance minister?'

'Yes, she's flying in tomorrow. She's a priest based in Carlisle called Helen Hughes.'

'That's great news! I have to say, though, I'm a lot less jumpy after another quiet night.'

'Me too,' said Alan, 'though I'll be happier still once Helen Hughes is here. She sounded very calm and considered on the phone.'

'Fingers crossed she can sort this out,' said Laura, looking out across the water.

'Agreed, though a few prayers might help too,' chuckled Alan.

'I'll leave those to you,' laughed Laura in return, before adding, 'Can I meet her?'

'I think it's important you do. I'll give you a call tomorrow once she's here to fix up a meeting.'

'OK, speak soon,'

'Aye. Bye for now.'

Dwight O'Neill was walking too, though not with his usual athletic stride. After a night during which he'd drugged himself to sleep with a combination of a bottle of Châteauneuf du Pape and two sleeping pills, he felt decidedly groggy. Shades covered his tired eyes as he negotiated the crowded pavements on his walk to work at the top of Wall Street. It usually took five minutes, but today it would probably be nearer ten.

It was a beautiful September morning of open blue sky and a soft, warm breeze, though Dwight didn't notice.

There were clouds scudding across his mind and, unlike the usual dreaded return after a vacation, he hoped that time back in the office might be just what he needed. With money and reputation on the line, the imperative to focus, as well as the company of colleagues, might give him the perspective to quieten the fears and confusion.

Seeing a positive in going back to work after a break was a first for Dwight. In fact, there'd been a few firsts in the last few days; his first panic attack at the airport and his first hallucination at the Jets game. Then last night he'd taken his first ever sleeping pills.

They'd belonged to a girlfriend who had lived with him for five months before he came home to find her things gone and a note on the kitchen counter saying she'd realised the only thing Dwight really cared about was himself. She'd left a few things in her haste to leave – some contact lens fluid and the sleeping pills, which had been in the bathroom cabinet, plus a pink thong that had caught behind a radiator.

At least the pills have come in useful, thought Dwight. He'd noted there were eight left. What was he becoming? He was now counting sleeping pills, hoping they'd help him get through a few more nights in a state of oblivion.

Then his mind looped back to the sailor he'd "seen" at the game. *Was it an hallucination? Some sort of subconscious guilt? The fact Gloria hadn't seen him would suggest it was. Or had it really been a ghost, like the Scottish woman talked about on Orkney? 'I see the dead,' she'd said. Could she? And now, could he? And was it all about the plate? Remi seemed fine and he didn't have a plate. Was the young guy, Callum, who took them out to the wreck,*

OK? He could ring him to find out. But what would he say? Wouldn't he sound plain weird just ringing up and asking someone on the other side of the Atlantic if he was OK when he hardly knew him? Then again, everything seemed to have become weird.

David Innes called the number Ally Flett had given him earlier for the sixth time as he ate his lunchtime sandwich.

'Hello.'

David bolted the ham and bread down and replied as if he was being choked.

'Hello,' he croaked.

'Hello? Are you OK there?' asked Shona Drever.

'Yeah, fine. Sorry. I was just finishing a sandwich.'

'Why did ye call if ye were eating?'

'To be honest, I wasn't sure you'd answer.'

'Why ring me then?'

It isn't a great start, thought David.

'Well, my name's David Innes. I'm the manager of the Scapa Flow Museum over on Hoy.'

'Oh yes. I know it,' said Shona, less guarded now.

'We've had a few strange things go on here. Oh, I am speaking to Shona Drever?'

'That's me.'

'Your name was passed on by Ally Flett from the Stromness Museum. I hope you don't mind me calling.'

Shona cut to the chase. 'You were talking about strange things happening. Is that in the museum?'

'Aye, and Ally said you might be able to help.'

'Well, tell me what's gone on and we'll see,' said Shona.

Remi Binks sat hunched intently over his computer, trying to pick up the threads of his work. He hadn't found his first morning easy or very productive after a week away, and his worries over Dwight kept resurfacing. The dream had really shaken him, and it brought back how odd Dwight had been after the *Vanguard* dive. This seemingly bulletproof guy had somehow changed overnight. What was it all about?

Remi looked at his phone, surprised to see it was well past noon. Dwight would be at work, like he was, so he decided to text – just a casual message that would give his dive buddy a route to help if needed, thought Remi.

Hi Dwight. How're you doing after the long flight home?
Shame about the Jets. I heard it was a great game.
Call me some time soon. Remi.

Dwight's phone pinged as he waited impatiently in the medical centre. He dug out the phone and read the message from Remi, shrugging to himself that he must have looked like shit yesterday for Remi to text him so soon after a vacation, before his mind moved back on to the issue with his hand. He looked at it closely, as if inspecting it one more time might explain why it had gone dead over the course of the morning. Before ringing the doctors, he'd even stuck a drawing pin in his thumb, drawing blood yet not feeling a thing. It had been scary and fascinating in equal measure.

His stomach rumbled, reminding him it was lunchtime and he hadn't eaten. He was relieved, however, that he'd been able to get a cancellation at his doctor's at less than two hours' notice. Dwight's irascible boss, Steve Rogers, all bald head and bombast, had not hidden his displeasure when he'd said he might be a little late back after lunch owing to a medical appointment. With luck though, Dwight hoped to be back on time, given that the doctor's surgery was only a five-minute walk from his office.

'Hello, Dwight, it's been a while,' said Doctor Kominsky, suddenly appearing in front of him, causing Dwight to look up with a start. The small, grey-haired, white-coated figure beckoned Dwight towards his office with a reassuring smile on his leathery face. Behind the smile, he had already noticed Dwight's hollow eyes and taut posture. *Drugs, drink, stress, or all three? Difficult to know with these Wall Street types,* thought Tomas Kominsky, who'd seen the physical results of corporate pressure so often in his thirty years as an MD in Manhattan.

Kominsky sat, swivelled, placed his hands across his stomach and smiled again.

'So, how can I help?' he asked.

'Well… er, it's my hand. It's gone numb over the course of the morning. Oh, and thanks for seeing me at short notice.'

'No problem, Dwight,' purred Kominsky as he leant forwards and took Dwight's meaty hand in his, turning it gently as he examined it.

'Can you move your fingers at all?'

'No. The most I can do is turn and bend the wrist. The fingers have stopped working completely.'

'Any trauma that could have caused it?

'Not really, just some diving on Friday where I felt a sort o' stinging pain in my index finger. I couldn't see anything to cause it, but it's gradually been goin' numb over a couple days, then this morning, the whole hand suddenly went dead.'

Kominsky nodded as he frowned in concentration while inspecting each digit in turn.

'Your index finger, you said? I can't see anything at all, but there is a puncture wound on your thumb.'

'Oh, I did that today. I leant on a drawing pin,' lied Dwight by way of explanation.

Kominsky frowned again.

'Do you feel unwell in any way? Any pain anywhere?'

'I'm a little tired after the flight and a few heavy nights.'

Kominsky smiled knowingly, before continuing to look at Dwight's hand, then his arm. He proceeded to take his blood pressure, pulse and temperature, before sounding his chest.

'Everything seems fine… though what's your usual resting pulse?'

'Sixty.'

'Well, it's nearer eighty today. That could easily be the partying and the flight though. Just wait here a moment, Dwight, I'm just gonna consult a colleague who used to specialise in muscular-skeletal issues.'

Once Kominsky left the room, shutting the door behind him, Dwight closed his eyes, only to snap them open again as the window blew outwards. Dwight felt a sharp, cold wind hit him, but from where? The door was closed.

The breeze seemed to envelop him, strong enough to ruffle his hair. As Dwight stared about him, seeking a cause, he became aware that his right hand felt icily cold, as if it was freezing from within. His fingers widened voluntarily, forming a rigid fan. He turned his hand over, examining it, scarily transfixed as warmth replaced the icy sensation, almost as if the cold was being drawn to his fingertips. Suddenly, the wind stopped and his hand felt warm. He waggled his fingers. They worked again, and when he pressed thumb to forefinger, full sensation had returned.

As Dwight sat open-mouthed turning his newly restored hand in front of his widened eyes, Kominsky re-entered and promptly slipped over, landing hard on his back, knocking the wind from him. He was followed in by another medic, who started helping him up.

'You OK, Tomas?' asked the younger medic as Dwight remained slack-jawed and silent.

'Uh, I think so,' replied Kominsky as he sat up, wincing.

'Hey, watch that water on the floor!' added the second doctor, noticing patches of wet.

'Looks like footprints,' said Kominsky, moving gingerly to his chair and looking at Dwight for an explanation.

Still dumbfounded, Dwight shrugged in response as Kominsky frowned before noticing the open window.

'It just flew open,' offered Dwight, following up with, 'I swear to God.'

'Well, maybe he's responsible,' said Kominsky dryly. 'Anyway, show Doctor Wilson here your hand.'

'Well, er, it's started to come back to life,' said Dwight weakly, avoiding the gaze of both doctors.

'What?' said Kominsky. 'Just now?'

'Yeah, I don't know why,' shrugged Dwight.

'Well, neither do we,' said Kominsky flatly. 'So, if there's nothing else, best you leave, huh.'

Dwight nodded, stood and moved to the door like an errant student dismissed from the principal's office.

'If the problem occurs again, leave it a few hours before ringing, OK?' said Kominsky, rubbing his elbow.

'Will do. Er, thanks, Doctor Kominsky.'

As Dwight exited, Kominsky looked at his colleague and raised his eyebrows, then both medics shook their heads in unison before the younger one took a towel to the floor.

'Always seemed like a regular guy when I've seen him in the past,' said Kominsky. 'Probably hitting the drugs hard. He's becoming psychotic.'

'Causing him to piss on the floor by the look of it.'

'Piss on the floor?' asked Kominsky, incredulous.

'Well, this isn't water I'm cleaning up. It smells.'

'What the…?'

Kominsky winced again as he leant forwards and carefully took the corner of the towel, sniffing it.

'That doesn't smell like urine though, Paul. That's sort o' briny, more like seawater.'

Tommy Walls leant his weight against the steel jemmy and the wood of the kirk's double door splintered before bursting open with a crack. Joe

Sandison gave a satisfied smile at his friend's efforts and looked over his shoulder to check they hadn't been seen, then they both ducked quickly into the vestibule. They stood on the chequerboard-tiled floor and looked around. There was nothing obvious to steal, just a carved umbrella stand and a glass vase of wilting flowers on a heavy wooden table flanked by two wooden doors.

That Monday afternoon, the two nineteen-year-olds had nowhere else to be and nothing else to do. They were two of a kind in appearance; thin figures in black hoodies that framed pinched, sly faces. Their prospects matched too, with both slipping inexorably down a slope of drinking and drugs since their final year in school. Notorious now in Kirkwall's shops and supermarkets as petty thieves, they'd been forced to try different means of funding their habits and a kirk sometimes provided easy, and occasionally lucrative, pickings.

'OK, in we go,' said Joe, pulling out a large shopping bag as Tommy opened the left door into one of the two aisles. They were met with a large, silent space of white walls, polished wood and coloured light from the stained-glass window above the altar. Again, they could see little of value, apart from what stood on the white-clothed altar with its cross and candlesticks and, of late, the two mess plates.

'Not a lot here, is there?' moaned Tommy as they walked to the altar while removing their gloves.

'These look like silver,' said Joe, fingering one of the candleholders then dropping both of them into the bag, followed by the cross, which landed with a clank.

They both then looked at the mess plates. Tommy

picked one up and turned it over. There was a blue scroll-like crest with the words "Fletcher-Miller" on it. It left them none the wiser.

'Must be for the collection,' said Joe.

'Aye, our collection,' laughed Tommy, passing it to his mate to put in the bag. As he did so, the plate felt suddenly warm. 'Weird! The plate feels hot.'

Joe touched it in the bag. 'Nae, it disnae!' he said, affecting a Glaswegian accent that he thought made him sound hard.

'Gimme it again,' said Tommy, touching it all over. Oddly, it now felt cold.

He then picked up the second plate, nearly dropping it into the bag as a searing heat scorched his fingers.

'Fuckin' hell. It's burnt m'hand!' groaned Tommy, as his fingers turned an angry red.

Joe frowned and carefully put a finger to the second plate.

'Nah, it's cold.'

'Bollocks it's cold! I've just burnt m'hand on it!' seethed Tommy, holding his hand under his armpit.

'See, Tommy. It's cold. Really!' said Joe, holding the plate up.

'What about m'hand then? It's burnt,' said Tommy, holding it out before his jaw went slack in puzzlement. His fingers had returned to their normal colour. The pain had also gone.

'Have you had anythin' this morning?' asked Joe, concerned he'd missed out on a fix.

'You know I haven't!' snapped Tommy. 'This is fuckin'

freaky. M'fingers were burnt and red and now they're OK. And don't tell me I imagined it, or I'll smack ye' one!'

Tommy's sharp voice echoed in the empty kirk. No sooner had it died than they became aware of a flapping sound behind them. When they turned to see what it might be, it was Joe's turn to gape in astonishment. The pages of the Bible on the lectern were flipping over with dizzying speed, sounding like a rattling fan.

'Come on, let's get oot o' here,' said Tommy, his eyes wide as he scurried towards the door into the vestibule. Joe didn't hesitate and was directly behind him.

They were soon outside, where Joe pushed the door closed as best as he was able to with the lock broken.

'Leave the stuff,' said Tommy.

'Nae chance.'

'You have it then.'

'Nae worries. I will,' said Joe, striding forwards, relieved there was no one around as they had come out. He moved quickly, the bag bouncing off his leg at times as he turned into a separate street of grey terraced houses with Tommy a pace behind. After a few minutes, Joe slowed to an amble, feeling they were far enough away now not to be seen as suspicious, though the raised hoods and rolling gait remained giveaways.

'What the fuck was all that about?' said Tommy as he fell in step with his pal.

'Must've been a window open to blow those pages like that,' offered Joe.

'That's shite and you know it! There was no window open anywhere. The place is fuckin' haunted!'

'Bullshit!' spat Joe.

'You saw it, Joe, same as me. And what about m'hand, eh? The plates being hot, then cold?'

'In your head, pal!'

'Fuck you!' said Tommy as Kirkwall Harbour came into view.

In response, Joe pursed his lips, stared directly forwards as if he were alone and picked up his pace once more. Tommy shrugged and let Joe move ahead as they crossed the road and walked along the dockside.

Joe swapped the bag from his right hand to his left. The weight of it had caused the handle to dig into his palm and he flexed his freed hand in relief as his mind churned over what had happened. He thought Tommy was on some sort of trip, talking about the plates being hot; they'd clearly been cold. But he couldn't explain the pages in the Bible flipping over. He couldn't remember any windows being open.

If he was honest with himself, it had been scary, and now he didn't really know what to do with what they'd taken. He wasn't sure he could sell it on quickly and knew he didn't want it under his bed at home in the meantime. He turned, waited for Tommy to catch up with him and held the bag up.

'Are ye' sure ye don't want it?' asked Joe with a placatory tone.

'Definite.'

'Well, I don't either. There's somethin' no' right in that Kirk. I'm not sure we can move this shite on easily anyway.'

'So, what're you gonna do with it?'

'Sling it,' said Joe, tilting his head in the direction of the water to his left and holding the bag over the black metal railings.

As he was about to drop the bag into the dock, he spotted some people exiting the Kirkwall Hotel further up on the opposite side of the road and knew dumping something in the water would look suspicious. There'd be a loud, noticeable splash too. So Joe walked on towards the concrete launching ramp that led into the dock. There he could get close to the water and slip the bag gently and quietly in when no one was looking.

Tommy realised what Joe intended to do as his mate walked down the edge of the ramp, bag in hand, so decided to stay at the top and keep a look out. From past escapades, Joe would know that if Tommy gave a low whistle there was someone watching; otherwise, he could carry on.

Joe approached the edge of the ramp, put the bag down and looked around. There was no one to be seen on any of the moored boats and as he glanced behind him, Tommy gave a quick thumbs-up. Joe reached down for the bag, but before he could grasp the handle, he felt a powerful shove in his back and was catapulted into the water.

Joe could swim but the cold bit into him immediately as he went under. His sodden clothes felt heavy too. Then his survival instinct kicked in and, with flailing limbs, he fought to the surface, gasping for air.

Tommy had been looking back towards the hotel when he heard the splash and lost sight of Joe for what seemed like a long time. When Joe finally resurfaced, he could see he was struggling, his arms thrashing the water with a clumsy, tired front crawl. Thankfully, there was a large orange lifebelt close by. Tommy urgently pulled it free and threw it in Joe's direction.

'Grab the bastard, Joe!'

Joe laboured towards the lifebelt, stroke by desperate stroke, eventually grabbing it. Relief replaced fear as Joe spat out a tired 'Yes!' when both hands closed gratefully around the ring. But it would be the last thing Joe would ever say. Suddenly and powerfully, he was dragged under.

Tommy's last sighting of his pal was of Joe's grasping fingers slipping from the large orange ring as if he was being pulled from below. He stared in horrified disbelief, watching the redundant life belt floating uselessly as he looked for a sign of Joe resurfacing. But Joe had gone, swallowed by the water.

15

Alan Muir was pleased he'd resolved to make it another alcohol-free night when two policemen knocked on his door at nine p.m. The more youthful of the two was carrying a large shopping bag.

'Good evening,' said Alan, almost quizzically.

'It's Reverend Muir, isn't it?' asked the older one.

'Yes.'

'We're led to believe that some items were taken from your kirk earlier today. We have them here if you'd like to confirm they're yours.'

'Oh, OK,' said Alan in surprise. He'd intended to check the kirk, specifically the mess plates, that afternoon but had been called to the bedside of a seriously ill parishioner and gone straight home afterwards, feeling drained.

The younger policeman brought out the first of the mess plates and held it up.

'Yes, that's from the kirk,' said Alan, regarding the plate almost fearfully now it was back on his doorstep.

'We've contacted a locksmith, Mark Jones, to repair the door. Have you heard from him?'

'No, no, this is all news to me,' said Alan, the reality of the kirk being broken into starting to register. It was the first time things had ever been taken.

'We'd advise you to nip down to the kirk to check the place over and ensure it's secured. We haven't been because we've caught who did it,' said the younger one with the bag as he replaced one of the plates in it and passed it to Alan.

'How did you catch them if they weren't at the kirk?' asked Alan, placing the bag outside the door.

'There'd been an incident down at the dock involving the perpetrators, one of whom was sadly recovered from the water unresponsive. There'll be an inquest to determine the cause of death in due course. The bag was found nearby. The one who didn't go into the water admitted to us what they'd been up to earlier,' said the older officer.

'And one of them's now dead?' said Alan, his voice reflecting his shock and concern.

'Unfortunately, yes,' offered the older policeman, before the younger one spoke up, almost eager to recount the bizarre happenings.

'From what we've been told, he was going to throw the stuff in the dock but fell in and went under. The other lad's in a terrible state, rambling on about the kirk being haunted and the Bible pages turning on their own! He's a regular drug user, which probably explains it.'

The older officer turned and gave his younger

colleague a glare, leading Alan to surmise he must have said far more than he should have.

'When he said the kirk was haunted, did he say he'd seen anything else?' asked Alan.

The slightly older officer cut in quickly.

'We didn't interview him, just picked him up from the dock as a 999 call. He was in a state when we reached him, as you'd expect, so he didn't make much sense. The stuff about the kirk being haunted was passed on from the custody sergeant. If you want to know more, I'd suggest you ring the station to see if any more information can be released at this stage.'

The final remark was said with a sharp stare at his younger colleague, who looked down, clearly knowing he'd overstepped the mark.

As soon as the police left, Alan looked in the bag to see what else was in it, then grabbed his coat and made for the kirk. It was only a five-minute walk and he felt he needed to do two things immediately: check on the building and put the plates back. There was no way he was keeping them in the house.

As he arrived, the light above the door illuminated a burly figure in a baseball cap working on the lock.

'Evening. Thanks for doing this so late,' said Alan.

The young man smiled and raised a heavily tattooed arm in acknowledgement.

'No bother. I would have got here sooner but the job I was on turned into a bit of a nightmare. This has been OK though. I'm nearly done.'

'That's good. I thought I'd get these things back to

where they belong,' responded Alan, holding up the carrier bag.

'The cops got them, then?' asked the locksmith.

'I believe so,' said Alan, keen not to be drawn in further. He stepped round the man and into the illuminated but cold vestibule.

'Oh, while I remember,' added Alan, 'how do you want paying?'

'I'll invoice you. Here, all done! There's two keys there. You'll need to get the wood repaired and painted before it rots as well,' said the locksmith, passing the keys over with a grin before exiting quickly.

Alan took a deep breath, opened the door into the kirk and reached for the light switches. Once the room was lit, Alan looked around slowly. His first impression was that there was no damage. It was a great relief, particularly in terms of the stained-glass windows.

He walked up the left aisle, looking at and between the pews. All seemed as it was before, save for the empty altar, but he soon remedied that, putting the plates where they'd been earlier, then replacing the cross and the candles, which he decided to light before sitting down on the front pew.

He regarded the small, yellow flames swaying slightly now and again, his only sense of movement in the stillness other than his own breathing. He realised he was at prayer, not with any words, just with a sense of being in God's presence. The plates held no fear for him in this place. In fact, nothing at that moment did. He had not felt peace like it for some time.

Eventually, Alan's mind began to wander. He looked at his watch – nine forty p.m. – then across at the lectern with the Bible on. He remembered what the policeman had said about the youth saying the pages had moved, something he too knew about, leading him to stand and see whether it remained on the verse it had flicked to when he was last here.

Though he wasn't completely surprised, his eyebrows still arched when he saw that the page displayed was no longer Proverbs. It was open instead at Ezekiel, where his gaze fell on two lines that looked as if they had been underscored by a fingernail, scratched heavily into the paper. They read:

"And I will execute great vengeance upon them with furious rebukes:

… and they shall know that I am the Lord when I lay my vengeance upon them."

Alan held the lectern and thought of what the policemen had said. Someone who had taken the plates was now drowned. Then his mind went back to Callum Craigie's crash. The young man was still in hospital for all he knew. This was no longer just bizarre and frightening; it was dangerous, deadly even, and Alan's sense of peace suddenly vanished. After saying a prayer for Callum and the dead man and his family, Alan mused that Helen Hughes could not arrive quickly enough.

Laura was sat at a picnic table in the courtyard of The Murray Arms, huddled into her fleece against the sharp night air. She was warming the stem of her virtually empty wine glass with fidgety fingers while savouring a cigarette when she heard a familiar voice.

'Hiya, Laura!' greeted Shona, who looked to be walking past. 'I don't normally drink in the week, but seeing you sat there, I think you've twisted my arm!'

'I've twisted nothing!' laughed Laura as Shona headed for the bar.

Shona was soon back outside, triumphantly holding two large glasses of white wine.

'Chardonnay OK?' asked Shona, smiling broadly.

'What are you like?' said Laura. 'I don't normally come down here in the week either, but it's a nice night so I thought I'd have one cheeky nightcap, and here you are leading me further astray.'

'I must have got alcoholic constipation from my grandad,' said Shona.

'What?'

'Alcoholic constipation. My grandad had it,' said Shona. 'He couldn't pass a pub!'

They both laughed at the corny line and clinked glasses, before Shona lit up herself, then looked serious.

'I think I'm getting somewhere with the plates mystery,' said Shona, blowing smoke through her nostrils.

'Oh, how?'

'I had a call today from the manager of the Scapa Flow Museum over on Hoy. They've had supernatural disturbances on Friday and Saturday night. A display cabinet messed up and the glass cracked. There's been wet footprints too, picked up on CCTV.'

'Really?'

'Yep. But then it gets more interesting.' Shona paused as she took a big gulp of white wine. 'The same thing happened in the Stromness Museum. But in both cases the display cabinets that were affected were for the same ship: *HMS Vanguard*.'

'So, it could be something to do with that ship?'

'It must be! Display cabinets in two museums on different islands both disturbed over the same weekend when closed. The dead sometimes try to communicate something to us. I'd bet this is to do with the crew of the *Vanguard*,' said Shona, her voice urgent.

Laura chewed her lip in thought, stubbed her cigarette out and took a sip of wine.

'So, where do you go from here?'

'Over to Hoy first thing in the morning. Wanna come?'

'Erm… OK,' said Laura after a thoughtful pause. 'Let's hope it's not too choppy.'

Dwight strolled slowly, almost aimlessly, among the throng in Times Square. A dizzying kaleidoscope of humanity milled around him, some with heads tilted back and phones pointing upwards as they gawped at the electronic billboards offering a continuous feast of colour and movement. He'd always loved the vibrancy, the scale, the proud gaudiness of Times Square. For Dwight, there was simply nowhere to match the buzz at the heart of New York City.

It was five thirty p.m. and he'd taken the subway straight after work to get there. It had been an odd first day back in the office, even if he discounted the scary and strange interlude at the doctor's. His work had thankfully kept him focused for much of the time and the familiar surroundings, routines and faces had been comforting, yet also strangely disconcerting. At first, Dwight couldn't fathom what was different. Then, as the image of the sailor at the Jets game kept reappearing in his mind's eye, he realised what had changed. It was him.

So, with a free evening stretching uncomfortably ahead, Dwight decided to head uptown. He aimed to lose himself in the crowd and the sights before finding food, then a bar, and seeing where the evening went. Wherever it took him, it had to be better than feeling caged by worry in his apartment.

He'd had two texts that morning. One was from his brother Michael about meeting up to shoot some pool on Wednesday. The other, from Remi, was unusual, though not in the circumstances. After all, Remi had been there when the problems started. In one sense, Dwight wanted to speak to him, to open up and tell Remi what was happening and how frightened and confused he had become. But Dwight had never done that. This new trend for sharing was for weaklings and losers, not for a real man for whom some laughs over a few beers with his buddies would usually put things right. So he had ignored the texts for now, preferring the distraction of the sights and of strangers to a meaningful conversation. At least his hand seemed to be better now.

'Hey, watch your feet!' said Dwight irritably to a large, middle-aged man in a red baseball cap who had stood on his foot while filming with his phone.

'Sorry,' said the man nervously, in thickly accented English. Dwight's first impression was that he was German.

'It's such an amazing sight, ya?' said the man, looking back up at the billboards.

Dwight gazed upwards too. As he focused on a giant 3D board, he froze. Looking down on him was the sailor from the Jets game with the same icy stare. His hand came up and seemed to point a giant accusatory finger straight at Dwight. It was as if the finger was moving ever closer to him. Dwight felt his stomach lurch. Then the image disappeared and an advert for a war film replaced it.

The German was no longer staring upwards. He had been checking his phone before looking sideways to see Dwight transfixed, his eyes wide and mouth agape. He looked up too in response, half expecting to see someone preparing to jump or a billboard ablaze, such was the fear in Dwight's face, but by the time the German looked, all he saw was the usual array of changing images and glittering lights.

'What can you see?' asked the German.

Dwight didn't answer. He just kept looking up, searching for the sailor once more. Concerned, the German touched his arm gently.

'Hello, are you OK?' he asked.

The man's touch seemed to break the spell and Dwight looked at the German, his eyes wild.

'Did you see him?' asked Dwight, urgently.

'See who?'

'The sailor!'

'What sailor?'

'The sailor that was on the screen, for God's sake!' shouted Dwight.

'I don't know what you mean,' said the German, confused.

'Don't play fuckin' mind games with me! He was there, thirty feet tall, pointing his fuckin' finger!' said Dwight, grabbing the man by the sleeve. The man recoiled in fear, pulling himself away and bumping into people behind him. Dwight turned to a young Asian man to the other side of him.

'Hey, you must o' seen him even if the blind Kraut didn't!'

The man backed away smartly, holding his hands up to signal he didn't want any trouble, but stumbled instead into a frail older woman, who shrieked as he trod on her ankle. Her partner shouted angrily and the young Asian yelled back, pointing at Dwight. They both began berating him, then two young women shouted at him too, simply keen to join in with harassing the rich-looking guy.

Dwight suddenly felt he was drowning in a sea of people; a swell of angry faces, loud voices, jabbing fingers and scuffling steps. His heart thumped and his head spun.

The developing commotion was noticed by a corpulent cop who strode over, his thumbs hitched into his belt like an old-time sheriff.

'Everything OK here?' he asked.

It was more a command than a question. He knew that announcing his presence was often enough to quell minor trouble. Then he noticed Dwight at the centre of the gaggle of people, all agitated movements and manic expression.

‘Excuse me, sir. Can I help you?’ asked the cop as he closed the space on Dwight.

‘These fuckers are playin’ mind games with me. The sailor was there! I saw him!’

‘What sailor, sir?’ enquired the cop. Dwight’s smart suit and shoes suggested a corporate type high on drugs.

‘The sailor on the billboard! I saw him with my own eyes!’

‘OK. Maybe these guys around you missed it because they were lookin’ elsewhere. There’s a lot to see up there,’ said the cop with a benign smile. He thought Dwight was probably high, or possibly a wack job. Either way, he needed calming down and moving away.

He took Dwight by the elbow and led him through the crowd, who parted, staring as Dwight was escorted to a quieter spot under the canopy of a restaurant. Normally, Dwight would have bridled at the thought of being led anywhere by anybody. But things were anything but normal now.

Dwight had begun to calm down and, after he was able to answer the cop’s questions about who he was and where he lived, both confirmed by his driver’s licence, he was advised to go home because he looked “dead beat”. As embarrassment rose above fear, Dwight nodded and walked awkwardly away, feeling spent. Part of him wanted to look back up at the billboards, yet he kept his head down as he trudged towards the subway. The truth was, Dwight was too scared to look up, and at that moment, too frightened to think ahead.

16

Laura savoured the fresh breeze and gentle motion of the ferry as they approached the small, spartan port of Lyness. She was relieved the crossing to Hoy had been a smooth one, knowing that wasn't always the case. Shona tapped her leg and pointed at the large cylindrical structure to the left of the landing jetty that looked like a massive grey drum nestling in rough grass.

'That's part of the museum. It's an old oil tank from the war,' said Shona.

'Only a short walk then,' replied Laura. Shona nodded with a smile.

Laura had done some online reading about *HMS Vanguard* that morning. She was amazed that over eight hundred men had died on the ship yet she knew nothing about it. She'd heard about the sinking of the Royal Oak in Scapa Flow in the Second World War even before she'd moved to Orkney, yet the destruction of the *Vanguard*, with a very similar death toll, seemed to be of far less prominence. To Laura, it seemed bizarre how two tragedies of similar magnitude could have such different levels of awareness.

This morning, she hoped to find out more about *HMS Vanguard*, though she was also a little apprehensive. Shona's talk of "supernatural disturbance" on the museum site, particularly after Alan had informed Laura last night that there might be a death associated with the plates, was unnerving. So, Laura was keen to stay as close to Shona as possible.

'Last drag before you get down to work?' said Laura, her face dimpling amiably as Shona lit up while they walked briskly towards the museum, a literal long stone's throw from the dock.

'And why not?' mumbled Shona, a cigarette balanced between her lips. 'Besides, you like a crafty little drag too, I've noticed.'

'That's the point. It's the odd one, not seven packets a week!' chided Laura with a gentle smile. Shona gave her a sideways look of feigned annoyance, then broke into a grin.

'Well, let's see what today brings, eh,' said Shona as they reached the door.

It was opened by a stocky young man with a strong, dark beard and a thick thatch of hair, beneath which kind blue eyes and a smile greeted them.

'Hi, I'm David Innes.'

'Hi, I'm Shona and this is Laura.'

Laura gave a slight nod and smiled as David reciprocated and they held each other's gaze. The mutual attraction had been instant and Shona noticed the pause before bustling through the door as David held it open for them.

'OK, then. Talk us through what's been going on,' said Shona, direct as ever.

'Probably best if I show you the display case.'

'Fine, lead the way,' replied Shona, keenly.

Alan Muir waited in the small airport terminal ready to wave his makeshift sign, a piece of cardboard with "HELEN HUGHES" written in black marker pen across one side. The deliverance minister's plane had landed and Alan expected her to step through the doors among the other arrivals from Glasgow at any moment. He was keenly anticipating her arrival, hoping desperately for some answers, especially after he'd received news of the death in the harbour yesterday.

As the passengers began to emerge through the "Arrivals" door, Alan held up his sign, then realised that his dog collar would make him easy to spot anyway. While he was deliberating whether to fold the sign up and stuff it in his jacket, he noticed a woman in jeans and a bright red jumper among the throng who was beaming at him and heading his way. She was small – clearly less than five feet – and slightly built, yet her easy smile and bright, kind eyes made a big impression. If Alan had been asked to age her, he would have struggled to answer confidently. While the laughter lines round her eyes and her grey hair, styled in a short, spiky crop, suggested she was well into her fifties, she moved with the fluency and energy of someone much younger.

'Hi, you must be Alan,' she said warmly as she approached him.

'Aye, that's me. And you're Helen?'

'I am,' she replied, extending a delicate hand with bright red nails.

'Welcome to Orkney!' said Alan, taking her hand in his sizeable fist, then offering his other one to carry one of her bags.

'Thank you,' she said, as Alan took the small, wheeled case, while she kept hold of a small rucksack by the looped handle. She followed him out of the terminal into a dry, bright day. As they walked the short distance to the car park, Alan didn't waste any time on further pleasantries.

'I'm really pleased you've been able to get here so quick. Things have become a lot more sinister since we spoke,' said Alan, slightly breathless as he dragged the case up the gradient to his car.

'Oh, how so?'

'There's been a death. Someone stole the plates that have been at the centre of the… er, happenings, and they've drowned in the harbour.'

'Really? How do you know the drowning's linked to the plates?'

'I don't for certain. But there were two of them involved in the theft and the one who's OK told the police the kirk was haunted. He was really spooked, apparently.'

'Sounds like we need to speak to him.'

'Agreed, but the custody sergeant wasn't giving me any information last night, so there's a job to do to track the lad down.'

Helen nodded as they reached the car and Alan placed both bags in the boot before they climbed in.

'Do you want to go straight to the kirk and see the plates?'

'Well, Alan, in a word, no. Ideally, I'd like a nice coffee and a piece of cake somewhere first. All I had on the plane was a small chocolate wafer!'

It was a blunt message but delivered with such a smile that Alan could only grin in return.

'That's not a problem at all. I know just the place,' said Alan, as he slotted the Focus into gear.

As Laura walked behind Shona and David Innes on their way into the exhibition area, she resolved to return in better circumstances. The museum certainly seemed worth another look, thought Laura, and if she was being honest with herself, so did the manager.

Through a set of heavy doors, they entered a dimly lit area where the first display on the left was dedicated to the *Vanguard*. Information boards showed photographs of the ship and its ill-fated crew underneath a splintered length of wood bearing the faded legend "*HMS Vanguard*". There was also a forlorn brass porthole with a lens of crazed green and yellow glass. Laura assumed the display case sat below it currently covered in a green tarpaulin. David pulled it forcefully from one end and it crumpled to the floor, revealing a glass case pock-marked and frosted with cracks. On closer inspection, the items in the case were also scattered about, almost as if they'd been ricocheting inside with great force. Laura had anticipated feeling frightened, though surprisingly she wasn't. Maybe the daylight and the company negated her fears?

'The wet footprints were there,' said David, pointing to the side of the display.

'And they happened just the once, you said?' confirmed Shona as she focused intently on the case, her eyes seemingly searching every inch.

'As far as we know. We cleaned them up on the Saturday morning and saw them on the CCTV from the night before, but haven't found anything like it since.'

'Can we see the footage?' asked Shona, still looking directly ahead.

'It's set up ready,' replied David with a grin.

There was a long period of silence as Shona stood in front of the cabinet, seemingly absorbing what was before her. Meanwhile, Laura sneaked a look at David, who, it turned out, had been looking at her first. They smiled simultaneously and looked away as Laura felt herself blushing.

'I sense great sadness here. A feeling of loss,' said Shona, finally looking at David.

'There's nothing missing though. We've checked,' offered David.

'It's not necessarily something from—'

Shona suddenly stopped speaking, furrowed her brow, then began walking towards the exit, evidently in her own world.

'Shona?' asked Laura out of concern, only for Shona to wave a hand dismissively while staring ahead and striding back towards the door. David and Laura exchanged puzzled looks and followed a few metres behind as Shona came out of the exhibition area, through the foyer, then out through the main door and on to the concrete concourse. She walked further still, past the outdoor exhibits and across the car park.

Finally, Shona stopped near the dock and looked intently out to sea as David and Laura caught up. Shona continued to ignore them and was nodding knowingly as if in conversation.

'What is it?' asked Laura as Shona began pointing out across the water.

'It's the *Vanguard*,' said Shona, 'The loss is from the *Vanguard* and I'll bet it's those bloody plates.'

'Why d'you say that?' asked David.

'Because a young sailor just guided me to here and pointed in the direction of the wreck. I know you can't see it from here, but it's somewhere over by the oil terminal,' answered Shona, reaching for her cigarettes.

Helen Hughes gazed up at the towering frontage of St Magnus's Cathedral, a takeaway coffee in one hand and a flapjack in the other.

'Impressive, isn't it?' said Alan.

Helen nodded and smiled, keenly surveying the solid, mottled sandstone of its walls and tower, before taking a sip of her latte.

'The coffee's good too! How about we grab that bench?'

replied Helen, walking carefully towards it to avoid spilling her drink.

Once they were sat down, they ate and sipped in companiable silence, people watching. There were certainly plenty to see. Many looked to be tourists, judging by the plethora of cameras and phones on show, invariably pointed at the cathedral.

After she'd finished her flapjack, Helen wiped her fingers carefully, slipped the serviette into her empty coffee cup and turned towards Alan.

'OK. To business. We'll start at the church – sorry, kirk – with a look at the plates and your flipping Bible, though I doubt I'll divine anything important from seeing them. I actually think it's more useful and important that I bless the houses where the disturbances have occurred.'

'That's easily arranged; one is mine and I'm sure young Laura will be fine about us going round to see her. I'll text her.'

'Is she in Kirkwall too?'

'No, St Margaret's Hope, down on South Ronaldsay, but it's only a twenty-minute drive.'

'Without further ado, then!' said Helen, jumping up from the bench. 'Get me to the kirk on time!'

17

Laura took a final look over her shoulder in the direction of the museum as the ferry pulled away from Lyness Dock on mercifully calm water. It had been another strange day. Only a week ago, she would have laughed at what Shona had said in the museum earlier, and thought the woman was mentally ill. Yet after the frightening happenings in her house, then seeing the state of the museum display cabinet and wet footprints forming on the CCTV, Laura was now convinced there was another dimension to life.

It was a relief to find out from Alan that the deliverance minister would be visiting the house later that afternoon at four. She'd not known whether to tell Shona about it, somehow feeling she might not like the idea, but when Laura did say something, Shona had welcomed it, saying mediums and clergymen were "on the same team, though some don't seem to know it". What Shona seemed more interested in was Laura taking David Innes's phone number in order to arrange a visit to the museum next week.

'No need to fret,' said Shona, 'you'll be back to see him soon enough, eh.'

'It's not like that!' protested Laura with a blushing giggle.

'Not like that, my arse! You couldn't keep your eyes off each other! And as for taking each other's numbers so you can visit the museum again – talk about a lame excuse! Anyone can go any time it's open. You don't need an appointment with the manager!'

'All right, I admit I liked him.'

'Liked him! I thought you were goin' t' trip over your tongue on the way in! I can just hear the wedding speech. "We bonded over our mutual experience of ghostly wet footprints"...' laughed Shona.

'That's not funny!' protested Laura, before joining in heartily and drawing curious looks from an older couple leaning on the boat's rail nearby.

Once the laughter died, Shona leant in towards Laura with a serious gaze and said quietly.

'After what's happened today, I'm goin' to need your help.'

'What do you mean?'

'Jean doesn't want me to see Callum, but we need to confirm for definite the plates are from the *Vanguard*.'

'I don't see how I can help,' said Laura.

'Well, he's a soft spot for you. If you see him, you can ask him where the plates are from.'

Laura sucked her bottom lip in thought, then nodded. If it helped to stop all this craziness, she'd try to speak to Callum as soon as she could.

Alan Muir and Helen Hughes stood on the grass banks enveloping the sunken stone dwellings of Skara Brae, transfixed by the remarkable stone furniture that looked as serviceable now as it had been five thousand years ago. They smiled in unison on hearing a small boy comment excitedly to his sister that it was "like the Flintstones". There was a definite element of truth in what the youngster had said.

'Photos don't do it justice,' said Helen, shaking her head in wonder. As a former history teacher, Helen had always wanted to see Skara Brae, so when Laura Matson had texted Alan back that morning to explain she was on Hoy and couldn't meet until the late afternoon, Helen had asked Alan to take her. As she strolled slowly round the site, she was certainly not disappointed by the settlement or the dramatic coastal setting.

Alan had been several times before, but the site always impressed and he enjoyed seeing Helen's enthusiastic reaction. She was certainly more animated than when she'd seen the plates in the kirk. To his surprise, she'd shown no reaction on seeing them and, once it was evident there'd been no further disturbance there, they'd moved quickly on to Alan's house, where she'd put on her purple stole before methodically blessing each room by sprinkling holy water and intoning a short prayer.

While he'd carried out similar blessings for parishioners,

it seemed so simple and unremarkable. To his mind, it somehow didn't match what was required given all he'd experienced. When he'd said this to Helen afterwards, she'd laughed, saying, 'God doesn't need a lot of bells and whistles to show his power', then immediately asked what they were doing about lunch. It had turned out to be prawn sandwiches at a place near Tankerness, where Helen had insisted on paying.

'What gets me about a place like Skara Brae is that even though this community existed five thousand years ago, we haven't changed that much. On a practical level, these people had their shelves and dressers, their sleeping quarters, just as we do,' mused Helen.

'But we're miles apart from them in terms of attitudes and beliefs, aren't we?'

'I'm not so sure. I just look at this settlement and see the humanity in it.'

Alan nodded, then said mildly, 'What about God, then? These people weren't Christians.'

'Does the fact they weren't Christians make a lot of difference?'

'If Jesus is "the way, the truth and the life", it surely makes a difference,' replied Alan.

Helen looked at Alan with raised eyebrows, though her easy smile stayed in place.

'These people worshipped in a way that made sense to them. Jesus wouldn't make an appearance for hundreds of years, so how could they do anything other? Do you think that made them lesser in the eyes of God?'

'Well, if they weren't Christian…' stuttered Alan.

'So what if they weren't Christian? See that little boy and his sister over there?'

Alan looked over at a family of four, enjoying the site. They were of Asian heritage and clearly Muslim, given that the mother wore a vibrant purple hijab over her hair.

'If you're saying the only way to God is through Christ, those kids don't have a chance then, do they? Is it their fault they're born into a Muslim family? By that reckoning, they could be morally upright people but still be off to hell regardless, while some corrupt TV evangelist can con money from people, yet they'll apparently be saved because they proclaim Jesus as Lord! To me that's just bollocks!' said Helen, her eyes aglow with indignation and her mouth forming as firm a line as her views, before the smile quickly returned and her gaze softened once more.

'Sorry, Alan. I didn't mean to get on a soap box,' she said.

'No need to apologise for a bit of honesty,' smiled Alan, before gazing out over the curving beach, where gentle waves spilled lazily on the shore. Helen moved closer and they looked out together, side by side.

'This is special,' said Helen, briefly closing her eyes and savouring the air as she inhaled. Alan stole a look at her. In the space of a few hours, a new force had entered his world, knocking him off balance one minute, delighting him the next.

'We can agree on that,' said Alan.

'And that we need to get to this young woman's house to do a blessing!' added Helen, suddenly businesslike again. 'We also need to think about how we might speak to this young man who broke into the kirk.'

'Aye, I've an idea on how we might get in touch with him. I'll tell you in the car.'

The theme from *The Good, the Bad and the Ugly* slowly seeped into Dwight's muffled consciousness, though by the time he realised it was the sound of his ringtone, the caller had rung off. He reached for his phone and groaned when he saw through bleary eyes that it was gone nine o' clock and the call was from Steve Rogers, the third one he'd made to Dwight since quarter past eight. As he swung his legs wearily off the bed and sat on the edge, the room seemed to spin momentarily and he felt sick. It was hardly a surprise given that he'd anaesthetised himself the previous night with a bottle of wine and three sleeping tablets for good measure when the prescribed dosage was two.

It had been another difficult evening. After the shock and humiliation in Times Square, he'd slunk away and ridden the subway down to South Ferry, where he'd bought a burger and fries from a street vendor on the waterfront. It was as much for something to do as for something to eat. Afterwards, he'd walked aimlessly around in the twilight, burping back the taste of onions and deliberating about when to go home.

There'd been more texts from Remi and his brother, both expressing increasing concern, but what could he say to them? He didn't understand what was happening to him, so how could he explain it? If he did say something, he thought he'd sound either certifiable or weak, probably both. As a result, he ignored the messages and walked miserably back to his apartment in the fading light.

Thankfully, nothing weird had happened overnight. Nothing he could remember, anyway. He'd drunk his way through Rocky III, a childhood favourite, before popping the pills and eventually crashing out. Hell, he couldn't even remember walking to the bedroom at the end of the night.

Now, Dwight had to face a new day, one that was beginning with a tricky call to his boss, a man who he once described to a new colleague as having two modes of operation, "difficult" and "fucking difficult". With a sigh, he worked his fingers over the phone screen and connected to the number. It buzzed twice before a sharp voice cut in.

'Where the hell are you, Dwight? It's past nine!'

'Yeah, sorry, Steve. I… er, I've been ill in the night and forgot to set my alarm.'

'Forgot to set your fuckin' alarm! This isn't high school, Dwight! How ill are you, for God's sake?' barked Steve. Dwight could see his round, red, angry face and his hand grasping the top of his bald head, as was customary when he became agitated.

'I'm feeling a lot better now. Must o' been somethin' I ate.'

'Well, get here, quick! You had your head up your ass yesterday, then went to see a doctor on your first day back in the office! Remember, Dwight, there's no passengers at Barton & Stowe!' berated Steve.

'Fuck you, Steve,' said Dwight after the call ended, before stomping wearily into the kitchen and squinting in the bright sunshine as he poured a large glass of water. He leant back against the sink unit as he drained the glass and his eyes naturally fell on to the mess plate sitting on the table. *Ever since he'd had it, things seemed to be unravelling. How could that be? It was just a plate, for God's sake.*

He picked it up, recalling how one of his fingers was so painful after he'd recovered the three of them from the seabed. He touched the plate all over, as if he was painting it with his fingers. He almost seemed to be urging it to hurt him again, then caught a glimpse of himself doing so in the reflection off the chrome of the fridge and stopped.

'I might be losing it, but even I'm not that screwed up,' he said aloud, before shouting 'Shit!' as he remembered the call with Steve. He headed quickly to the shower and was soon gasping under the first hot jets of water. Once showered, shaved and dressed, Dwight felt more awake and his competitive instinct resurfaced. He'd show Steve who had his head up his ass.

He was reaching down for his shoes in the hall when he noticed them – a set of wet footprints leading to the kitchen. Yet he'd gone straight to the bedroom next door after his shower. Cautiously, slowly, Dwight walked to the kitchen, his heart beating hard and his eyes wide. The door was open and he scanned the room quickly as he entered. No one was there, though the footprints continued up to the table.

His eyes fell on the plate just as two things registered simultaneously; it was brimming with water and there was a strong smell of brine. He looked up. There was no leak from the ceiling and all the windows were closed. *What now?*

Dwight shook his head and his mouth twisted in

anguish. He crept forwards to the mess plate, eyes locked on it as the water rippled like a small, windswept pond. Then he peered into it, his hands grasping the edge of the table for support.

The water moved, becoming dark and cloudy, with swirling greens and blues like those of the sea. Dwight stared through frozen, frightened eyes as the shades and colours changed and coalesced into a vision that made him cry out. It was the sailor – the one he'd seen at the Jets' match and in Times Square – looking out from the plate, his angry face just below the surface. He mouthed something that Dwight couldn't lip-read.

'What?' asked Dwight, desperation in his voice.

Then the face emerged from the water and Dwight recoiled, crying aloud again, before looking back to see the sailor's head grow and rear out of the plate as drips spilled across the table. His fierce, blue eyes blinked away water, or were they tears?

'Send me back,' said the sailor. It was a young voice with a soft, Scottish accent.

Dwight watched, mesmerised, as the head shrank before sinking slowly back under the surface, holding his gaze until it disappeared into the dark water as if descending into the ocean depths. He kept staring into the plate, where the water gradually cleared and became still once more.

Dwight shook his head and blinked rapidly as his heart hammered a terrified beat. How could it be real? Then he put his hands out and touched the droplets of water on the table before sniffing his fingertips. It was the smell of the sea.

After what seemed a long time, though was less than five minutes, Dwight finally moved away from the table while keeping his eye on the plate. He then moved quickly to the closet to retrieve his rucksack. On his return, he took a deep breath, grabbed the plate, drained the water from it in the sink and placed it in the bag.

Breathing quickly, adrenaline coursing through his trembling frame, Dwight called Steve Rogers.

'Dwight? Where are you?' asked Steve irritably.

'I'm still at home, Steve. I've been thinkin' it over and I've decided I'm not comin' in.'

'What? You...'

Dwight didn't hear what Steve went on to say next as he loudly rode over his words.

'I'm not comin' in. Period! I'm not wasting another minute working my ass off for a cheesedick like you. Fuck you, Steve!'

At that, Dwight ended the call and took a deep breath before putting his shoes on, hooking the rucksack over his shoulder and walking out of the flat. He felt he knew where he must go and the sooner he was there, the better.

18

Laura followed Helen Hughes from room to room, fascinated by the process of blessing the house. She'd been impressed by Helen's clear concern and the way she'd listened so intently to her description of what had happened the previous Friday evening.

'Can you sense anything, Helen?' asked Laura as they returned to the kitchen, where Alan had made a pot of tea.

'No, but I rarely can. Sometimes people tell me they can see apparitions and I can't see anything,' shrugged Helen.

'Couldn't they be mentally ill?'

'Yes, and I believe that's the case sometimes. But take your situation and Alan's – some hauntings, or whatever you call them, are clearly real. I can also think of a recent case where three people in the same family could all see a figure in their garden and I couldn't see it, but I'm convinced from their reaction and the fact they appeared otherwise so normal that something was there.'

'Are you ever frightened?' asked Laura, taking a mug from Alan with a grateful nod.

'Sometimes, but God's on my side so I know that ultimately, I'll be OK. Mind you, I've been shaken up a few times when something's surprised me.'

'Such as?' enquired Alan.

Helen took a sip of her tea as she thought about it.

'Well, there was a time I was in a house when a glass ornament that was on the mantlepiece disappeared. When we went into another room, it was on a table.'

'Could it have been an identical ornament?' said Alan.

'That was my first thought, but it was a glass fish, old and scratched, and it looked exactly like the one on the mantlepiece. Besides, the one on the mantlepiece disappeared as I was looking at it with no one stood nearby!'

Helen took a biscuit from the plate with a smile. It was as if she'd been recalling an event from a holiday or some similar mundane anecdote.

'What else has shocked you?'

'Seeing things move in the air, though it's very rare to see. I once saw a small electric fire hovering in the air. The bars were glowing orange and giving off heat, yet it wasn't plugged in. That was certainly a strange one!'

'And what's the most dangerous thing you've been involved with?' asked Laura, fascinated.

'That's hard to say. Supernatural activity can harm in ways you can't see. Physically, I've seen people sustain injuries from things being thrown around, but I've thankfully never encountered a violent death. That's what makes this case potentially so serious, because we don't know why that young man crashed his car, nor why another poor youth has drowned. In both cases, let's hope they're not to do with the plates.'

'Aye,' said Alan concernedly, recalling the intact plate in Callum's wrecked car.

'Aye indeed,' replied Helen, 'because if they are linked to the plates, this is new territory for me too.'

Remi looked at his phone with a worried frown. He could see that his text had been delivered to Dwight, yet there'd been no response, yet again. He'd tried calling too, leaving an answerphone message.

'Hey, Dwight. Just ringing to see how you're doing, buddy. Give me a call just to let me know you're OK. Remi.'

Remi had given up for the time being and was just re-focusing on his work on the screen when his phone pinged. It was a message from Dwight.

Hi, Remi. All good here. I'll call you later.

Remi's brow knitted and his eyes narrowed as he read it. The message should have reassured him, for some reason it didn't. If all was "good", why hadn't Dwight texted that earlier? Remi punched at his phone in response.

Good to know all is OK. Look forward to catching up.

He sucked his lip as he heard the electronic swoosh of the text being delivered, hoping his sixth sense about Dwight was wrong.

Dwight heard his phone 'ping' and looked almost absently at the text from Remi. He'd sent a reply to Remi's voicemail to try to stop the messages, without knowing if he really would call later. So much seemed to depend on what happened when he reached his destination today.

He rocked gently in his seat, locked in his own world, as the half-empty train sped underground towards the upper East Side of Manhattan. It was a prosperous area, the one he'd been raised in, and where the church of St John Vianni stood.

Dwight's parents were devout Catholics and raised their boys in the faith, so both had duly taken Holy Communion aged ten before drifting away from the Church in their early teens. Through the mists fogging his mind, Dwight tried to remember the last time he'd been there; his parents had since moved to Long Island. It was probably his uncle's funeral fifteen years ago, when old Father Michael was still the priest. He was probably long gone by now.

Father Kevin Duffy rubbed his eyes and let out a long yawn as he pushed himself back on the castors of his office chair and away from the computer screen that had been holding his attention for much of the morning. The weekly newsletter was largely complete, though he'd wait for any further news before sending it out on Friday. With that task done, he was ready for something to eat. He hauled his bulky frame out of the chair and stalked towards the small kitchenette adjoining the church office, where he kept his usual lunch – a chicken mayo sub he invariably bought on his way in. It was something in an otherwise cheerless day to look forward to, along with his regular coffee and cookie breaks.

It had all felt so different six years before when Father Kevin became a first-time priest at St John Vianni, before six years of sad hours spent at the bedsides of the dying, countless church thefts and a dwindling congregation had sucked the spiritual zeal from him, now evident in every round-shouldered sigh and dragging step.

As the kettle clicked off and he poured the hot water in to the cup, he heard the loud thump of the church door close, meaning it had been opened and someone had entered. He cursed the fact he'd forgotten to lock it, knowing that his confessional slot wasn't due to start for another hour, and hoped it wasn't another thief or drug addict. It was probably too warm today for it to be a vagrant who would invariably be happy with a short stay out of the elements before he moved them on, occasionally with some cookies as a bribe if they looked like they could become aggressive.

Father Kevin walked through the back rooms and into the large, high-ceilinged space of the church to see a tall man stood in front of the altar. He wore a smart blue suit and brown brogues and was hugging a rucksack to his chest. As Father Kevin approached, he could see he had a wild look about him; red, tired eyes and a tight, tense expression.

'Can I help you?' asked the priest, eyeing him warily, wondering in particular what the rucksack contained, fearing it might be a weapon of some kind.

'I hope… I, er… I need help. God's help, I think.'

'Well, my friend, you're in the right place for that,' said Father Kevin with a forced smile, still keeping his distance, uncertain of Dwight's intentions.

'Can I sit down? I'm really tired,' asked Dwight.

'Sure. Take one of the pews. May I ask what's so precious in the bag?'

'It's a plate. It's why I'm here,' said Dwight, removing it from the rucksack and holding it up, before taking a step back and sitting on the front pew, placing the plate beside him.

'What's special about it?' asked Father Kevin, moving closer but still maintaining a three-yard distance. The guy was big, after all, and bitter experience had taught him not to get too close to random visitors.

Dwight took a deep breath as he tried to think about how to start to explain something he couldn't fathom himself.

'It's a mess plate from a shipwreck. I took it – I dived to the ship and took it – and I shouldn't have and things have been getting weird ever since. It's… er… it's like I'm being haunted by this sailor. He's everywhere. He was sat on the bench at the Jets' game, then he was on the billboards in Times Square, and today…' Dwight's throat tightened as he recalled what he'd seen, strangling the voice from him, as his eyes leaked tears and his mouth moved without making a sound.

The guy isn't likely to be a threat, thought Father Kevin.

He's just mentally disturbed. Yet another nut off the New York production line who always seem to find their way to St John Vianni.

Dwight was trying to think, grasping for the right words amid a storm of fears and feelings.

'This is my church!' said Dwight loudly.

'Sure. It's everyone's church,' schmoozed Father Kevin.

'No! You don't understand! I took my Holy Communion here!' shouted Dwight.

Father Kevin took a half-step back.

'OK. So how about I bless your plate and you can be on your way, er…?'

'Dwight. I'm Dwight O'Neil. My parents came here for years. It was our church.'

'OK, Dwight. Put your plate on the altar for me and I'll get some holy water.'

'But will that send him back?' asked Dwight, almost child-like.

'Send who back?'

'The sailor! That's what I'm tryin' to tell you! The sailor came out of the plate saying, "send me back",' said Dwight impatiently, his voice growing louder again as he became more agitated.

Father Kevin was losing patience himself – and he was hungry. *The guy was certifiable and the sooner he was through the door and it was locked, the better.*

'If the plate's haunted, blessing it will send him away,' asserted Father Kevin, his expression authoritative. Dwight nodded and blinked repeatedly. It was what he needed to hear.

Father Kevin walked to the nearby font and filled a small flask with water, then proceeded to the altar, where he took hold of the plate while keeping Dwight in his field of vision. He turned to face him as he held the plate in one hand and flicked holy water on it with the other, while reciting a perfunctory blessing in a flat tone. He caught a glimpse of his watch as he did so; it was now past twelve thirty and his stomach was rumbling.

'That's it, Dwight. Go in peace, my man,' said Father Kevin with the smile of a salesman.

'It's done? That'll send him back?'

'Almighty God can do anything.'

'Of course. Er, thanks,' said Dwight, unsure what to do next, only for Father Kevin to quickly hand him the plate and manoeuvre him down the aisle and out the door in a fashion more akin to a security guard than a priest. His chicken and mayo sub was waiting, after all, and he'd just remembered he'd saved a jelly donut from yesterday too.

As the large door closed behind him, Dwight blinked in the sunlight, uncertain how he felt and still struggling to think with any clarity. *Was it really over? The priest had said so, so it must be, mustn't it?*

After a few minutes standing there trying to order his thoughts, he decided to text Remi and let him know. It might stop him calling.

Hi Remi, I've had problems with the plate, but I've seen a priest today and he said the sailor has been sent back. All good now.

Remi had been away from his desk making a coffee when the text from Dwight pinged on his phone. His mouth dropped open and his eyes narrowed once again as he read it. In fact, he read it several times, wondering if he could spot any obvious predictive text errors, or if the message really was what Dwight intended.

After a thoughtful pause, Remi started clicking his mouse with a quick, practised hand and soon located the phone number for Barton & Stowe, where he asked to be put through to Dwight O'Neil, telling the receptionist he was an old customer. The phone simply rang out. Dwight didn't appear to be there, as Remi had suspected.

So Remi tried a different tack, ringing reception again and asking to speak to Dwight's "line manager" as "a matter of some urgency". It worked and Remi soon heard the sharp tone of Steve Rogers.

'Hello. Can I help you?' asked Steve. Remi sensed a hint of impatience.

'Hi there. Hopefully you can. My name is Remi Binks. I'm not actually a customer but I need to know if Dwight O'Neil is OK.'

There was quite a long pause before Steve spoke again.

'And who are you in relation to Dwight O'Neil, Mr Binks?' asked Steve, his words dripping caution.

'I'm a friend.'

'Well, all I can say is that Dwight resigned this morning. I'm sure he'll speak to you about it in due course.'

'That's just it, I need to track him—'

'Good day, Mr Binks,' said Steve curtly, before the connection was cut and Remi sat chewing his lip, stunned by the news that Dwight had left his job. It just didn't fit with how driven he was, unless he had something else lined up, but he'd said nothing when they were away and was definitely prone to over-sharing.

'You OK?' asked his colleague Tom, who was eating a sandwich at the opposite desk.

'Yeah, I'm OK, but someone I know probably isn't. Looks like I'm gonna have to ask the boss for a couple days off.'

'Hell, you've only just come back off vacation!' said Tom.

'I know, but I don't think this can wait.'

Laura walked briskly towards the Craigies' house on Front Road, thinking about what to say. The light was fading while the wind was picking up. Sharp gusts whipped Laura's hair irritatingly across her face as she tried to rehearse her words. Her concern was Callum getting the wrong idea about her visiting, so she'd decided to say she was there to pass on Alan Muir's best wishes.

She felt conflicted about not telling Alan about her discussions with Shona and been dreading him asking about her trip to Hoy, but he didn't mention it, so neither did she. Despite Shona's comment about priests and mediums being "on the same team", Laura wasn't sure how Alan or Helen Hughes would receive what Shona had said, particularly after going to Hoy. Then again, she knew that if Helen Hughes was to sort this out, she needed to know everything there was to know. Laura resolved to ring Alan later, once she'd seen Callum and possibly knew a little more.

On reaching the door, she took a deep breath and knocked. Jean soon opened it with a welcoming smile.

'Laura! Are you here t' see Callum?'

'Yes, I've a message to pass on from the man who got him out of his car.'

'Come in, hen,' said Jean, ushering her to an armchair in the lounge.

Callum was on the sofa in his regulation grey hoodie and jogging pants, plumped forwards on a pile of cushions with Lady curled up next to him, his hand on her side. The small collie lifted her head and wagged her tail briefly on seeing Laura, then put her ears down and closed her eyes once more as Callum gave her head a stroke.

'Hiya, Laura,' grinned Callum through swollen lips.

'Hi. How are you doing now?' asked Laura, shocked to see the long, sutured scar down his nose between bruised panda-like eyes.

'I'm OK. You should see the other guy!'

All three of them gave a slightly forced laugh, before Jean disappeared into the kitchen to make a pot of tea.

'I'm here to pass on Alan Muir's best wishes,' said Laura after an awkward pause when Jean left the room.

'Alan Muir?'

'He was the guy who pulled you out of your car.'

'Oh, the priest? Aye, well, can you thank him for me?'

'Will do! He'll be pleased to know you're home too.'

'How come you know him? He's not from South Ronaldsay, is he?'

'No, he lives in Kirkwall. I've got to know him a bit the last few days because of the plate you gave me.'

'The plate?'

'Yes. Some strange things happened the night you gave it me. I passed it to Alan Muir and he had weird stuff happen too.'

'What sort of stuff?'

'Noises, smells, wet footprints, things you can't explain,' said Laura, searching his face for clues as to what he knew. Callum put his head down, avoiding Laura's gaze, as Jean returned with a pot of tea and cups on a tray.

'I know he looks a bit of a sight, Laura, but he's thankfully in one piece. And he'll be good as new after a bit o' rest,' said Jean, looking fondly at her son. 'It could've been worse. Look at that poor lad drowned in Kirkwall. It's all over the front o' *The Orcadian*.'

'Aye, Joe Sandison. I knew him from school.'

'Did you know he had the mess plates?' asked Laura.

'What?'

'Him and his mate had apparently taken the plates from Alan Muir's kirk just before he drowned,' said Laura, her face serious and the underlying message clear.

As Jean busied herself with the tea, Callum was silent and Laura felt awkward, so focused on Lady sleeping peacefully as a distraction. When she looked back at Callum, his face was contorted, as if in pain. Tears started to roll down both cheeks and his shoulders began to rock. He then let out a long groan that turned to sobs.

'What is it, hen?' said Jean, putting her hand on his shoulder as Lady began to lick the tears from his cheeks.

It was a while before Callum's shoulders stopped shaking and he was able to speak.

'I'm sorry,' snivelled Callum. 'I should never have given you the plate.'

Callum looked at Laura, his eyes puffy and pained, while his bottom lip trembled like a child. Laura could only feel sorry for him.

'Hang on! You're both just buying all this bloody ghost stuff hook, line and sinker. How d'you know for certain that's what's going on?' said Jean.

'Because I didn't just come off the road, like I said in the hospital!' moaned Callum loudly. 'The steering wheel was wrenched round in m' hand! It was like someone had grabbed it and forced me off the road!' Jean's mouth dropped open and she started blinking rapidly.

'You weren't to know what would happen,' offered Laura.

'No, I didnae. But taking those Yanks to dive on the *Vanguard* was out of order.'

'*HMS Vanguard*?' shouted Jean. It was an exclamation as much as a question and Callum nodded miserably at his mother. Any vestige of doubt that what had been happening was supernatural Laura held on to evaporated. She was now certain all Shona had said was true.

'What were they doing diving on the *Vanguard*?' asked Jean.

'They paid me to take them. I wasn't to know that one o' them would be stupid enough to pinch stuff off the wreck.'

'Those plates?' asked Jean.

'Aye,' said Callum, head down.

'So, Shona was right,' added Laura.

'I'm not following it,' said Jean.

'I went with Shona to the Scapa Flow Museum over on Hoy yesterday because their *Vanguard* display case had been smashed up. Shona made the connection between the mess plates and the ship, saying all the problems were linked to *HMS Vanguard*.'

'How much were you paid?' said Jean. Callum kept his head down, then Jean shouted, 'How much? Let's have some honesty, m'lad, at last!'

'Five thousand,' replied Callum quietly.

'Five grand!' roared Jean. 'I'm bloody ashamed! And as for what your dad's going to say…'

'Callum wasn't to know what would happen,' repeated Laura, but Jean's hard expression didn't change.

'No, but he was brought up to know that breaking the law and disturbing a war grave is wrong all day and every day!'

'What now?' asked Callum with a sniffle.

'I'll let Alan Muir know about what happened with your car if that's OK. He's brought a deliverance minister over from England to try and sort out the, er… hauntings.'

'What, like an exorcist?' asked Jean, eyes wide.

'I suppose so, yes,' said Laura. 'She blessed my house earlier on today.'

Jean and Callum both nodded gravely as Lady looked from one to the other with worried eyes, sensing the tension.

'I think Shona needs to know too,' said Laura.

'Aye, she does,' said Jean with a rueful look. 'I'll speak to her. I owe her that.'

Alan and Helen walked slowly along the terrace of grey houses, eyeing the numbers closely in the twilight as they searched for 23. It was a shabby street of yellowing net curtains and paint-blistered doors, a five-minute walk from St Magnus's Cathedral, yet a world away.

'You did well tracking this lad down,' said Helen.

'Orkney's a small place and as a priest, you cross paths with a lot of people.'

They smiled knowingly in unison.

Alan had found Tommy Walls's address through one of his parishioners, Billy Ross. He'd become a Christian in Barlinnie Prison, having served time for burglary to feed a drug habit. Now, as a clean, reformed character with a new life on Orkney as a builder, he volunteered at a youth centre in Kirkwall and had come across Tommy there. Billy had spoken to Tommy's mum on Alan's behalf to explain he would not be pressing charges but would appreciate the chance to speak to Tommy. She'd agreed at once, relieved to hear Tommy wouldn't be in court once again – though whether Tommy would be happy to speak to Alan and Helen remained to be seen.

'Number 17… 19… these are odd numbers on this side. It's just up here,' said Helen.

'Aye. Let's hope he's in.'

Following Alan's knock, there was only a short delay before the door was opened slightly and a bottle-blonde woman with a thin, careworn face peered round it. On seeing their dog collars, she widened the door.

'You must be Reverend Muir?'

'Aye, that's me, but call me Alan. And this is Reverend Helen Hughes, who's working with me at the moment.'

Helen nodded and smiled before saying, 'Please, call me Helen. And you must be Tommy's mum?'

The woman gave a resigned smile. 'For my sins, aye. I'm Kirsty, by the way. Come in. Tommy's in the lounge.'

They followed her into a short, woodchipped hall where they were assailed by a pervading smell of cigarette smoke, then through into a lounge where Tommy sat in a threadbare armchair in an equally spartan room, scrolling on a phone. He looked up briefly when they entered, then looked back down at his screen, avoiding eye contact.

'Hello Tommy. I'm Alan Muir and this is Helen Hughes. Thanks for agreeing to see us.'

Tommy gave a perfunctory shrug and kept his head down and his lips sealed.

Alan continued. 'Can we both say we're sorry to hear about your friend, and sorry for your loss. He was a lifelong pal, I believe.'

There was a pause, as if it took a few seconds for Alan's words to penetrate, then Tommy looked up, his eyes red and raw.

'Aye, pretty much. I'd known Joe since I was five,' said Tommy. His voice was thin and sad.

Alan and Helen nodded empathetically, then waited. Their experience told them there was nothing they could say to help the situation. A few seconds later Kirsty put her head round the door and filled the silence.

'They were two little so-and-sos together, I can tell ye, but Joe was a good friend to Tommy right enough,' she said, adding, 'I think Tommy's got something he wants to say to you Rev… er, Alan.'

'Sorry,' said Tommy quietly, 'and er, thanks for not pressing charges.'

'Well, normally I would, but after what's happened to Joe and with you handing the items you took in to the police, it seemed the right thing,'

Kirsty smiled from the doorway as Tommy looked at Alan briefly and gave a small nod of gratitude.

'From what the police said, it sounds like you had a frightening experience,' said Helen.

'I did, aye.'

'Tommy, the reason I'm here with Alan is because I'm a deliverance minister. That means I deal with strange events, supernatural things, and it would help us a lot if you can tell us what happened to you and Joe, if you feel you can,' asked Helen, compassion in both tone and expression.

Tommy fiddled nervously with his phone for a few moments before sitting back and looking at them. Then he began.

'We broke into the kirk looking for stuff to nick and sell on. We took the stuff from the altar but that's when things went weird. I picked up this plate and it felt hot, then when Joe touched it, he couldna' feel anything. Then it happened wi' the second plate and this time it fair burnt m'hand, I could see my fingers all red. Then I put m'hand under my arm in pain, then when I looked at it again, my fingers were normal and the pain had just gone. Again, Joe touches the plate and it's cold. We had words, him makin' out I'd been on something when I hadn't. Then it was the book on the stand, the Bible, isn't it?' said Tommy, shaking his head, still struggling to comprehend what he had seen.

'What happened with the Bible?' asked Helen.

'The pages started flipping over like crazy. That's when we ran and ended up down by the dock. We were proper spooked, so Joe went down the ramp to sling the bag o' stuff in the harbour. Next thing, I hear a big splash and he's in the water. I threw him the lifebelt and he got to it, but then he just went under… and that was it.'

Tommy's face crumpled and he sat forward, head down again, leaking silent tears on to the carpet.

'Something grabbed him, I know it did!' cried Tommy. 'He had a hold o' the ring, then he just went straight down… gone! But the police, they weren't interested. We're just a couple o' scallies on drugs to them. But I'd had nothin, not a spliff, nothin', and I know what I saw both in the kirk and at the dock.'

'What do you think you experienced, Tommy?' asked Alan this time.

'In the kirk, some sort o'ghost thing I suppose, maybe making things happen because we were stealing stuff. With Joe, I don't know. It couldna' been a shark or a whale because when they found him they just said he'd drowned; no marks on him. But I do know he was pulled under. By what?' Tommy shrugged. 'Anyways, what do you think?' he said, looking at Helen.

'I think there's some sort of spirit linked to the plates, given that two other people have experienced strange things, one of whom is Alan. He saw the pages of the

Bible flip over on their own too, so you're not imagining it, Tommy.'

Alan duly nodded before Helen continued.

'As for what happened to Joe, I know less about that than you, so I can't say anything other than to repeat that I'm sorry for your loss.'

'Me too, Tommy, and if you ever need someone to talk to or even shout at, you can call me. I also know Billy Ross would be happy to speak to you,' offered Alan, passing him a card with his details on as Tommy nodded a thank you.

Helen had gone silent, though her mind had begun to race. She knew now that they were on dangerous new ground.

19

Helen was relaxing back on Alan's sofa when she heard his phone ring in the kitchen and Alan pause his cooking to answer it. She heard him say "Laura", so assumed it was the young woman whose house she'd blessed earlier. She hoped there'd been no untoward developments.

It had been an interesting day in a place that was new to her and she'd enjoyed a great deal of it, particularly meeting Alan and visiting Skara Brae. The house blessings had also appeared straightforward.

Yet Helen now had an underlying sense of unease. The idea of supernatural forces possibly drowning a young man wasn't an easy thing to contemplate. More to the point, she still didn't know how to go about dealing with it, and after a long, eventful day she wasn't in the mood to think or pray with any real focus. Hopefully, a good night's sleep and a new day might bring more clarity.

Helen was scanning the news on her phone when Alan called her through to the kitchen. He'd clearly gone to some effort, judging by the tablecloth, serviettes and immaculately set cutlery.

'Wow! This looks good,' said Helen.

'Let's hope it tastes good too,' Alan replied, carefully carrying a chicken casserole to the table before returning with another pot full of vegetables.

'There's no starter I'm afraid, but there is plenty.'

'I can see that.'

'Would you like some wine?'

'Yes, please.'

Alan poured a glass for Helen before filling his own with water.

'Do you not like wine?'

'I do, but I'm, er… not drinking at the moment,' said Alan, shifting a little in his seat.

'For health reasons?' asked Helen. Her direct gaze was warm and knowing.

'Truth be told, I've been hitting the bottle. It'd been brewing, excuse the pun, for a while I suppose.'

'I've known it happen to a few people.'

'Aye, I'm sure. But the scare I had with the strange goings-on with the plate, it brought me up short. Really made me think.'

'Fair enough. It's an easy trap to fall into.'

'It is. And for me, one drink quickly leads to another these days, so I'm trying not to have any at all at the moment.'

'To be honest, I did wonder,' said Helen.

'Why's that?'

'Oh, I just have this extra sense sometimes.'

Alan stopped piling vegetables on his plate and looked at her, intrigued.

'Yes, it's called spotting two whisky bottles in the recycling,' said Helen, eyes twinkling, before she began to laugh. Alan soon joined in, off balance once again, but enjoying every unpredictable minute.

The rest of the meal was a combination of wholesome food and flowing conversation. Politics was discussed, politely at first, then more robustly as they relaxed in each other's company. They shared a mutual dislike of the Tories, though Alan said he thought Helen's Green Party leanings were a wasted vote compared to one for Labour, who Helen described as "Tory Lite". On music, though, they were closely aligned as Fleetwood Mac and Bruce Springsteen devotees, discovering to their delight that they'd seen 'The Boss' at the same concert at Old Trafford in 2005.

They also spoke about family. Helen listened with moist eyes as Alan talked of losing Alison and she gave a knowing, sad smile when he mentioned his son Ben, distant these days in all respects. She'd then said "snap", explaining that she hadn't seen her son Gareth, who lived in Vancouver with his Canadian partner, in over four years.

Alan broached the subject of Gareth's father delicately before Helen answered bluntly. Paul, her former husband, had in effect done a "trade-in for a newer model", as Helen put it, ten years ago. Although she'd been devastated at first, Paul had now been "well and truly replaced by Colin".

It took a few more minutes of conversation for Alan to happily establish that Colin was a cat.

With the table cleared, they went into the living room, tired and full of food. Alan put 'Born in the U.S.A.' on the CD player at a low volume as Helen cradled her wine, curled her legs under her in an armchair and looked serious for the first time that evening.

'Did I hear you talk to Laura earlier when you were getting the food ready?' asked Helen.

'Aye, you did. I was waiting to tell you what she'd said once we'd finished eating.'

'Why's that?'

'I didn't want to spoil the meal.'

'That bad, eh?' said Helen, raising her eyebrows and taking a sip of wine.

'Well, a concerning development. You've been busy all day and I wanted us to have a break from it all, to be honest. There's nothing we could do tonight anyway,' said Alan, seeking to explain himself when he didn't need to.

'OK. What development?'

'Laura went to see Callum, the lad I pulled out of the car wreck, who gave Laura the plate and had the other one himself. Well, he told her today that he didn't crash on purpose – a force, like an invisible hand, had turned the steering wheel and sent him off the road.'

Helen shivered though the room was warm, and she exchanged a long, searching look with Alan. Both could see that the other was shaken.

'Powerful stuff,' offered Helen finally, draining her glass.

'There's more.'

'Go on.'

'Laura's been speaking to a woman where she lives who claims to be a medium. I came across her when she got into an exchange with a loud American and I calmed him down. Apparently, this woman – Shona, she's called – had said to the American that she'd seen the ghost of a sailor stood behind him and he flipped.'

'Hardly a surprise!' laughed Helen.

'True! Anyway, today this Shona went to Hoy with Laura, to the Scapa Flow Museum. The museum had called Shona in because they've had damage to a display case for the ship *HMS Vanguard*. It had been messed up. The display case for the *Vanguard* has also been messed up at the museum in Stromness, apparently. When they were on Hoy, Shona claimed that a sailor, a ghostly one that is, pointed to the wreck site of *HMS Vanguard*, which is near to Hoy.'

'Hold on, you're going a bit fast,' interjected Helen. 'This *HMS Vanguard*, what's the story behind it?'

'It blew up in the First World War in Scapa Flow. Hundreds were killed. It's a war grave.'

'Right,' nodded Helen.

'But the important bit is that the mess plates are from *HMS Vanguard*. Callum got the plates from the American divers he took out to dive on the wreck. They paid him handsomely – five thousand pounds for a clandestine dive. Then they stole the plates from the wreck site.'

'So, the cause of the haunting is the theft of the plates?' said Helen, arching an eyebrow.

'Looks that way.'

Helen was quiet for a moment, fiddling with the stem of her glass, deep in thought, then said. 'It does sometimes happen that supernatural activity occurs when something is disturbed – a gravestone, for example. Why not items from a shipwreck? One thing that's odd, though – we saw Laura this afternoon and she'd been to Hoy. Why didn't she tell us all this earlier?'

'She was worried we'd frown at the idea of her involving a medium.'

'Well, I know a lot of clergy would steer well clear of mediums, sometimes with good reason, but to me, it looks like this Shona's done more to sort this out than anyone else,' smiled Helen. 'I think we have to see her.'

'Agreed. And it all fits with what she's said. The singing I heard, like the crew of a ship, and the face in the water in the plate, the briny smell, everything.'

'So, tomorrow we need to meet up with this Shona if we can,' said Helen. 'Is it too late to ring Laura now?' She looked at her watch and saw it was nearly eleven o' clock.

'I think so,' said Alan, rising from the sofa. 'And besides, if I leave this any longer, I'll be too tired to do it.'

'What's that?'

Alan punched buttons on the CD player and the pumping, urgent sound of 'Dancing in the Dark' started filling the room. He walked over to Helen and held out his hand. She took it with a smile and, as they began to dance, they cast aside the cares of today and tomorrow, immersed instead in a heady mix of nostalgia and delight.

20

It was just after three o' clock in the morning when Laura awoke fully after a fitful five hours of moving around the bed in various positions, none of them evidently restful. Having looked at the clock before letting out a frustrated sigh, she listened intently, wondering if she'd been woken by a noise. She heard nothing other than the familiar rustle of a large shrub under the window being buffeted by the wind. Yet there was still a vestige of edginess after her strange experiences on Friday last and Laura decided to get up just to make sure all was as it should be in the house.

Having put the bedside lamp on, which caused her to screw up her eyes, Laura padded barefoot to the bedroom door and listened without breathing for a few seconds before opening it and quickly flicking the hall light on. It was quiet, though she still checked for wet footprints in the hall before making her way to the kitchen and pouring a tumbler of water. She looked about her as she sipped. Everything was as she'd left it and she returned to the bedroom after a toilet stop, where she scowled at her puffy-eyed reflection in the bathroom mirror.

Once back in bed, Laura lay there restless with thought. What Callum had said about his car being forced off the road and seeing his fearful reaction had certainly unsettled her, particularly after hearing about the death of someone who had stolen the plates. While she knew that could just be a coincidence, it might not be, and the worry settled on her like a dark cloud on a mountain.

She wondered what tomorrow would bring. Helen Hughes seemed pleasant and confident, but Laura wondered what they were going to do with the plates. Given what Shona had said on Hoy, it seemed likely they'd take them back to the wreck of the *Vanguard. But how would they do it? Just throw them over the side of a boat? Hire a diving team?* She also thought about the American who Shona said had a ghost standing behind him. *Had he taken other things from the ship? Had anything untoward happened to him and his mate, or couldn't the ghosts travel, as it were?* Eventually, sheer tiredness swamped Laura's stream of thought and she began to snore softly.

'This seems crazy,' said Kim, as Remi Binks packed a few things in a rucksack placed on their bed. 'And besides, we can't really afford it.'

'I know that, but there's something wrong with Dwight. I can just tell.'

'How?' challenged Kim. She was sitting back against the headboard of the bed with her knees drawn up, her voice low to avoid waking Holly.

'He's quit his job, he's not answering his phone, then sends a really strange text I don't understand. It's just not the Dwight I know,' said Remi, placing his washbag in the holdall.

'But how well do you know him? You've been diving with him a few times, that's it.'

'Yeah, but he's usually an open-book kinda guy and something's off.'

'Like what? You're not making a lot of sense here, Remi,' huffed Kim.

'Well, he went a bit weird after the final dive – shouting in his sleep, fiddling oddly with his hand, then he had a panic attack at the airport. It was like an instant personality change,'

'Sounds like a breakdown.'

Remi nodded, continuing to squash things in his bag as Kim continued.

'But that isn't really your problem, baby. He has family in New York, right?'

'A brother,' said Remi.

'So, let him sort it out.'

'Kim, I just gotta go,' sighed Remi. 'My gut feeling is… well, Dwight needs help and his brother might not be around. Besides, I bought the plane ticket and it's only a day.'

'Your gut feeling is costing us two hundred and fifty dollars we don't really have. Then there's taxi fares, food!' hissed Kim.

'I know, but if I don't go and something bad happens… I don't think I can live with that,' said Remi.

Kim looked at Remi's worried face and her expression softened. He was a good man and usually a sensible one. She knew that if he felt the need to spend money that squeezed them and annoy his boss by taking a day off work straight after a vacation, he wasn't doing so lightly. She just hoped the trip turned out to be worth it.

Text messages swam fuzzily in front of Dwight's tired gaze as the metro train rocked its way South beneath the streets of Manhattan. It had been another bizarre day. He'd committed career suicide and visited a church for the first time in years, from where he came out feeling hopeful rather than guilty as he always used to. He felt a lot better after the plate was blessed, yet the mental fog hadn't fully lifted.

In response, he'd spent the day visiting old haunts. He'd listened to the high-pitched yells and squeals from the yard at his elementary school, stood outside his parents' old house, where the door was now red instead of Jets' green, walked in Central Park like he did as a kid, and ate pancakes at his family's favourite diner.

He was trying to re-connect to himself but, though the memories were clear, it was if they belonged to someone else. The cord between past and present had snapped somehow.

Thankfully, the sailor seemed to have gone. The visit to the church had been worth it. Maybe now Dwight could start to refocus and rebuild, though his evening spent chugging several beers alone in a noisy bar meant he would start on that tomorrow. The mission now was to get home, pop a few sleeping pills and hope for temporary oblivion.

It was just after eleven and the train carriage was a third full, passengers dotted around its seats singly or in small groups. Dwight was in an empty row of four with two shady-looking young characters directly opposite. One was olive-skinned and hunched, looking at the world with small, darting eyes from beneath a Yankees cap. The second was stocky with a widow's peak of dark bristle, ear spacers and an equally vacant expression. Though behind soulless eyes, he was making his calculations. *This blond dude is guarding this bag so must have something worth stealing in it. Could be a laptop. He's big but looks like a white-collar type, he'll be soft from spending his time doing deals and counting his money. Besides, he looks half out of it, drunk, stoned, perhaps both. It's an easy hit for two of us.*

In normal circumstances, Dwight would have sensed potential danger, but he was far from normal at that point. So, when he reached his stop at South Ferry, he was oblivious to them following him off the train. They kept ten yards behind as he made his way out of the station and began closing in where it was darker, beyond the electronic eyes of CCTV.

Dwight heard a series of quick, scuffling steps before they moved beyond him and blocked his path. There was a click as Dead Eyes opened a flick knife and held it up with a cold smile.

'Gimme your bag, dude, and you won't get hurt,' said Yankees Cap.

Dwight had the city experience to know that resisting in these situations was a massive risk. Taking on two men with one, or possibly both, carrying a knife was a crazy thing to do. But at that moment, Dwight simply didn't care. He'd had another weird day and now these two punks thought they'd screw him over and take his plate. *So, let's see them try.*

Dwight threw a right cross with all his might, which crunched into Dead Eyes's nose, shattering bone and sending him crashing down, where his head hit the floor with a sickening crack. Then he kicked out wildly at Yankees Cap. His hard leather shoe found the cartilage in his knee, splitting it in two. He went down with a scream while his partner in crime lay senseless at his side.

'Motherfu—' said Yankees Cap, before the word died in his throat as Dwight delivered a kick to his chin, knocking him out cold. He looked down at the two inert figures, chuckled to himself, picked up the knife and strode away, before throwing the blade into undergrowth near the path.

Dwight was grinning manically as the adrenaline surged through him. It seemed to suppress the beers and befuddlement and he felt alert, fully alive. *Man, he'd just taken those punks apart inside three seconds.*

The exhilaration couldn't, and didn't, last. His system began to slow as he walked on, tiredness set in and his hand began to throb. As he approached the apartment block, his thoughts turned to the sailor once again, though he comforted himself with what the priest had said earlier in the day. *It was over,* he told himself, *all over.*

Once inside, he reached for the tablet bottle from the kitchen counter, then found some frozen peas for his swelling right hand. He kicked his shoes off, walked through to the bedroom, sat on the bed and placed the cold, lumpy bag on his knuckles.

While waiting for the peas to do their work, he decided to kill some time by reading the two texts he'd noticed when he put his things down. He saw that one was from his brother Michael just as the balcony light blinked on. It glowed orange through the full-length curtains, beyond which Dwight could look down on the people of Lower Manhattan from a leather recliner.

As Dwight's gaze was drawn to the balcony, he subconsciously began to hold his breath at what he saw: the silhouette of a person perched on one of the chairs. His heart began to hammer as he sat, transfixed by the outline of the seated figure just yards away behind the curtain. Whoever it was clearly wore a distinctive hat. In shadowed form, it made their head look T-shaped. Dwight grimaced in fear as he recognised it as the headpiece of a British sailor.

After a minute or so, he jumped up, flicked on the light and scuttled towards the curtains, urgently pulling them back, revealing two empty chairs in a pool of amber light. He walked on to the balcony, where the tiles were cold under his feet and the muted thrum of a half-asleep city drifted up from the streets. He looked around wildly as his heart continued to race, then moved back into the bedroom, where all was still.

As Dwight shut the glass doors and sat back on the bed, the full realisation of what was happening to him exploded within. His body shook, his head dropped into his hands and he did something he hadn't done since childhood. He cried out in fear. It was a desperate, whimpering, frightened cry that went on for some time with no thought about being heard. After all, being heard didn't matter anymore. Dwight was trapped, confined to a tormented world where neighbours, reputation and self-respect counted for nought.

When he replayed in his mind what he thought he'd seen, Dwight was sure the silhouetted figure's head had tilted back, the mouth open and the shoulders shaking as if in malevolent mirth. Despite what the priest had said, the sailor had returned – but he wasn't crying this time. He seemed to be laughing instead, enjoying Dwight's suffering. What had he become? Dwight O'Neil, the big New Yorker who always had an answer for everything, could see no way out.

21

Helen moved the curtain to reveal a rain-smeared window, beyond which the day had dawned wet, blustery and grey. She'd slept soundly despite the frightening news regarding Callum's crash and after fifteen minutes of contemplative prayer on waking, Helen's mood was almost surprisingly light. She still had no definite answers but was content they would come. For now, a shower and some breakfast was all Helen needed. She was also looking forward to seeing Alan.

Laura bent forwards into the wind, rain stinging her face as she walked along Pier Road towards the ferry terminal. She viewed daily walking almost like pleasurable therapy, though today it felt more like a job of work as she blew the water that continually dripped down her face from her mouth. She squinted out over the sea wall at the shallows to her right, carved into sharp, speckled patterns by the elements before disappearing under a curtain of grey mizzle fifty metres from the shore.

HMS Vanguard came to mind. Its remains lay not far away in Scapa Flow, a sunken graveyard for so many vessels, and Laura wondered what it might be like to dive to such a ship, to see its massive, mangled shape, changed by nature and time. Laura wasn't even a good swimmer, but in that moment, she had a sense as to why the Americans had paid Callum handsomely for an illegal dive. Curiosity, exclusivity, mystery, the sheer thrill of venturing into the unknown. Laura thought they were all probably part of the motivation that subsequently unleashed such frightening events. *But what of the Americans and the third plate? Had they left the problems in Orkney or had their lives been upended too?*

Alan had been just as busy making a cooked breakfast as he had been making the evening meal, resulting in another enjoyable time together at the kitchen table. Helen had remarked that the pile of food she'd been served begged the question whether she was to eat it or climb it, eliciting a loud laugh from Alan that would prove to be the first of many that morning. The laughing stopped, however, when they entered St Magnus's Cathedral.

Though Helen's coat and jeans were drenched following the short walk from the car park, she became oblivious to her damp state as she looked around her. The warm, red stone of the pillars flanking the aisle and the pale, coloured light filtering through the stained glass seemed to emanate a sense of calm to Helen. Alan looked fondly at her as she gazed upwards, her eyes creasing as she smiled. She seemed to drink life in.

'It's beautiful, isn't it?' said Alan quietly, as if hushed by the majesty of the building.

Helen nodded, then walked slowly down the aisle before alighting on a pew near the altar. She'd left the end one vacant and looked round at Alan as if inviting him to join her, which he did. As they zipped open their coats, a woman did a double-take on noticing their dog collars.

After sitting silently for a few minutes, Alan leant into Helen and whispered, 'The last time I was in here, I overheard a young boy say to his mother, "I feel small and big at the same time."'

'Isn't that the idea?' Helen replied.

'Aye. It sums it up. We're so small and temporary compared to this place, yet each of us is so important to the God it was built for.'

'You think it was built for God? I think it was built for us,' smiled Helen, before she closed her eyes. Alan followed suit and in the transcendent beauty, a feeling of peace settled upon them as if they were being prepared for what was to come.

Shona arrived at Roberston's Coffee Hoose at exactly one o' clock, a little breathless after walking up the slope of Church Road. As she sucked the air in and her chest heaved, the sharp breeze tugged at her thick grey frizz, though Shona paid it no heed. She was just happy it was dry after a morning of solid rain, during which Jean had turned up at her door drenched and downcast.

A long heart-to-heart between the two sisters followed, in which Jean had apologised for not seeing that Shona had Callum's best interests at heart. Shona had responded with a hug, more tea and a generous plate of biscuits. It was a big hole mended, leaving Shona feeling so much better as she savoured a cigarette on the pavement.

Within a minute, she spotted Laura walking briskly down the road on the opposite side. She too lived only a short distance from Robertson's and enjoyed their excellent coffee as much as Shona liked the cakes. Laura grinned on seeing Shona, then raised her hand in acknowledgement at a dark Ford Focus turning into the adjacent car park. Shona then recalled that it was Alan Muir's car she'd seen occasionally near The Murray Arms.

Within a few minutes, polite introductions had been made and they were sat round a table covered in coffees and assorted cakes, easing into each other's company with talk about the weather. As the conversation flowed, Shona looked over the rim of her mug and admired the deep purple of Helen's clerical shirt as she removed her coat. Matched with her jeans and walking boots, her easy style and kind eyes were encouraging signs that they might just get along.

It wasn't long before talk turned to the strange events that had brought them together and they quickly agreed the theft of the mess plates had probably caused the hauntings. The solution was equally obvious. They needed to return the plates to the ship. When Shona said it, everyone nodded.

'So, how do we do that exactly?' asked Laura.

'I can speak to Callum. He'll know someone who can take us,' said Shona.

'If I'm to be included in this, it will involve me performing some religious rites,' stated Helen with an enquiring look at Shona.

'I'm easy with it, despite a priest once telling me I was an instrument of the devil! To be fair, I've no problem wi' the church; it's the church that's got a problem wi' me,' said Shona with a shrug.

'Fair enough,' said Alan mildly, indicating an understanding had been reached.

'The question now is, when do we go?' asked Laura, realising once she'd said it that 'we' meant she would be involved, even though she wasn't entirely sure she wanted to be.

'How about today, now the rain's cleared?' offered Helen. 'No time like the present!'

'I can ask Callum and see what he can do but I doubt he can find us a boat and a crew just like that,' said Shona.

'It's also quite windy,' said Laura with a grimace.

'But the wind's due to drop,' replied Shona, 'so, let's see, eh?' She moved her thumbs quickly over the screen of her phone in order to ring Jean.

'Oh, and if we're going near to Hoy, it might be an idea that I bless the museum too,' said Helen.

'Laura will give you a way in there,' smiled Shona with

a wink at her younger friend. Laura's face coloured and she grinned shyly.

'What about the Stromness Museum? Haven't they had some problems too?' asked Laura.

'They have, but I doubt Ally Flett will be bothered about it being blessed. Knowing him, he's probably revelling in the idea that his museum's haunted!' laughed Shona.

Remi looked out at the soft folds of cloud stretching for miles below the aircraft as he sucked his lip in concerned thought, fingers rapping on the arm rest. He'd tried to ring Dwight once again before the flight to New York, then left a voicemail and sent a short text, both asking his dive pal to ring him "soonest". Remi knew he'd sounded worried on the voicemail. He was worried, after all, and he hoped Dwight might respond to that. Then Remi remembered what Dwight was like.

Dwight woke slowly, his mind clanking into gear like an old steam engine after another drug-and-alcohol-induced sleep. When his thoughts started to become coherent and he realised where he was and what his last memories were from the night before, his stomach lurched from a sense of dread. The bolt of adrenaline made him want to move, though his eyes were still shut and he didn't want to open them, frightened of what he might see. His hand hurt too, and he remembered the street fight, though with no satisfaction now.

Eventually, he blinked and looked upwards at the ceiling, before slowly sitting upright. The bedside clock read nine thirty-three a.m. Thankfully, there were no sailors to be seen and no strange noises or smells, only the familiar faint hum of traffic from the streets below and the occasional sound of a helicopter chopping the air as it ferried the corporate barons between skyscrapers.

Where to now? thought Dwight. Even in his numbed state, he recognised it was a bigger question than whether to leave his apartment that Wednesday morning. At that minute though, getting out of what felt like a haunted cell seemed the obvious thing to do. So, he began to change into the first things he saw on the wardrobe shelf: black jogging pants and a red sweatshirt. He didn't want to risk going into other rooms so forewent teeth cleaning and a wash, moving cautiously instead from the bedroom to the hall, then into the kitchen, noting with relief that there were no wet footprints.

As he drank orange juice from the carton, which tasted bitter on the back of his throat, Dwight's eyes fell miserably on the rim of the mess plate peeping from the rucksack on the counter. Without knowing why, he grabbed the rucksack, his phone and keys, impatiently forced on some trainers without undoing the laces and retying them, then walked woozily out of the door.

He moved to the lift while glancing at his phone and saw there were messages from his brother, his dad and Remi. He stopped and closed his eyes, swaying on the spot. Dwight didn't want to talk to anyone. He didn't want to think hard or explain anything. All he wanted was to escape from the sailor, but he didn't know how.

22

The *Peedie Star* cut through the calm waters of Scapa Flow under a largely open sky, swaying slightly in the gentle breeze. It carried six passengers seated on the white benches running down its length in two rows of three. Alan, Helen and Laura sat on one side, while Shona, Jean and Callum faced them. All looked clumsily bloated in their yellow life jackets, except the seventh person on board – the skipper for the day, Gary Bremner. He was in the wheelhouse, steering a course to the wreck site of *HMS Vanguard.*

Callum had wanted to take them, but Jean had insisted he wasn't well enough, though did relent on him going if she went too. Gary had fortunately been on a day off and Callum's offer of a thousand pounds to take them soon moved him from his sofa to readying the *Peedie Star* for the trip. Jean had raised her eyebrows when she overheard

Callum offer his friend such a large sum, though was pleased to hear him explain that the money from the Americans had "caused nothing but trouble, so it may as well do some good".

'I can't believe it's the same day as this morning,' said Laura.

'Well, you know what they say in Orkney; if you don't like the weather, wait an hour,' laughed Shona.'

'Wait ten minutes, more like,' said Callum, and they all chuckled.

Alan looked across at Callum, who had the plates next to him in a canvas bag, within which they'd been wrapped in a Union flag akin to a sea burial. Ideally, they would have liked the plates to have been returned to the ship by divers, but at such short notice, none could be found. They'd all agreed instead that sending them down to the wreck in a flag was the next best thing and preferable to waiting for an available dive boat and risking further untoward events.

'Are you going to do the honours and put the plates over the side, Callum?' asked Alan.

'I'd like to, if that's OK with everybody,' said Callum, his swollen mouth forming a crooked smile. There were approving nods all round.

Helen had already blessed the plates after they'd been wrapped and sprinkled holy water on them from St Magnus's Cathedral. She was now preparing for a deliverance prayer at the wreck site, reciting the words in her head as she placed the purple stole round her shoulders, draped over the life vest.

'Colour clash!' exclaimed Shona with a laugh.

'Oh, I don't know,' said Laura, 'purple and yellow can complement each other.'

Helen smiled but she felt increasingly tense. This was something beyond her experience. So, she responded as she always did in such circumstances: she prayed. There weren't really any words; she was just trying to engender a sense of trust, of handing the situation over to God, and it calmed her. As she refocused on the world, Alan gently touched her arm. Callum was pointing ahead at a black and yellow buoy, bobbing gently like a small metal pyramid, two hundred metres or so away. They were closing on *HMS Vanguard*. The mess plates were almost back where they belonged.

With fifty yards to the buoy, the engine dropped an octave and the *Peedie Star* began to slow. Gary turned and looked at Callum, then drew a small circle with his finger, indicating that he would go round the wreck marker and stop. Callum explained what they were going to do to the group and as the buoy grew larger, Helen could feel the adrenaline pumping. In response, she pulled the deliverance prayer card from her pocket. She'd said the prayer many times, knew it by heart and rarely made reference to the card, but having it to hand made her feel better.

The buoy was soon within virtual touching distance and Gary stilled the engine. The group became silent, as if awed by what they knew lay beneath them. The only sounds were the slight slap of water on the boat's side and the rhythmic, eerie creak of the buoy on its chain.

Helen and Callum, who were both sat nearest the stern, stood up, each ready to play their part. Then, things suddenly changed. The *Peedie Star* reared upwards at the bow, lifted by a massive swell that caused Helen and Callum to topple backwards. Alan instinctively reached out and grabbed Helen's foot, while Callum was pitched into a foaming, heaving sea to the sound of Jean and Shona's screams.

As the *Peedie Star* swayed and bucked violently, those onboard gripped whatever fixtures they could. Jean continued to shout Callum's name and look wildly round her, trying to spot him among the jumping waves. Helen lay on the floor, stunned, with one hand on the bench and the other holding on to Alan.

As he prayed fervently and gripped Helen's boot, he could feel the water spraying on to his back, as could Laura and Shona, who could do nothing except hold on. Meanwhile, Gary Bremner fought to stand upright and start the engine before his head smashed into the wheelhouse door, knocking him senseless.

Callum knew he was in trouble as soon as he surfaced, gasping from the cold. Even with a life jacket on, he was being tossed like a rag doll in the swirling tumult. He could hear his mother screaming his name, then the only sound was the rush and glug of water as he went under. It felt as if someone had grabbed him by the ankles and was pulling him down.

Laura tried to stand and help Gary, but lurched forwards instead, landing on Shona, who pushed her back on to her seat, shouting, 'Just hold on, or you'll go over the side!'

Laura gripped under the bench again as water began splashing into the boat, soaking Helen, who slowly rose to her knees like a floored boxer trying to beat the count, before crying out to her God.

'Christ within me,
Christ behind me,
Christ before me,
Christ beside me,
Christ to win me,
Christ to comfort and restore me.
Christ beneath me,
Christ in quiet,
Christ in danger,
Christ in hearts of all who love me,
Christ in mouth of friend and stranger.'

Bubbles of air had begun to leak from Callum's mouth. Tantalisingly, terrifyingly, he could see the rolling surface a few feet above yet seemed to be held fast, however much he struggled. Just when he sensed he could hold on no longer, he popped to the surface like a cork from a bottle. Gasping and relieved, Callum greedily drew in the air over and again, amazed to be back at the surface, where he could see the waves were subsiding. Then he heard a shout and recognised his mother's voice. He turned round in the water and saw the *Peedie Star* was only about forty yards away.

Laura was tending to Gary, who was propped up against the wheelhouse, thankfully now conscious and able to talk. Shona smartly stepped over them, started the engine, spun the wheel round and headed towards Callum. She was clearly no stranger to boats.

Meanwhile, Alan murmured a prayer of thanks before helping a bedraggled Helen on to a bench, where they held on to each other from a mixture of shock, relief and burgeoning affection. After a minute or so, Alan spoke.

'Calming a storm. Isn't that in the Bible somewhere?' he said with a half-smile.

Helen nodded with half-lidded eyes, as if exhausted, before saying, 'It wasn't down to me. It's all about Him upstairs.' Then she added, 'I was still bloody scared though!'

'I think we all were,' he replied.

After a shout from Jean alerted him, Alan jumped up to pull Callum back on board once Shona had cut the engine. Callum's clothes made him heavy, but after some hard, grunting effort, he was heaved back over the side with the extra help of Jean and Helen.

As the water dripped from him, Callum sat breathing heavily for a long time. Eventually, his eyes fell on the mess plates, which hadn't seemed to move throughout all the turmoil. Alan followed his gaze and wondered aloud.

'What do we do with them now? Put them overboard?'

No one spoke. The heaving sea seemed to have cowed them into indecision. Then Shona's voice boomed out from the wheelhouse.

'No! We can't. It won't finish it. That's why the sea boiled up, I'm sure.'

'Why d'you say that?' asked Helen.

'Because when the boat started to heave, a voice said to me, "It's not complete", over and over again,' said Shona, emerging on to the deck.

'What voice?' said Laura, helping Gary on to a bench.

'The sailor's voice. The one I heard at the museum.'

'So, what does "not complete" mean?' she asked.

'Well, there were three plates taken. We've only got two and the way we were thrown around for five minutes out of nothing is a pretty strong message to me,' said Shona.

There was a short silence before Helen spoke. 'We've no other ideas. I suggest we go with what Shona's saying. That means finding the other plate, and in the meantime, we take the two we've got back to Alan's church.'

'But how're we going to get the other plate? It could well be in America!' said Jean.

'I've got the Yanks' phone numbers,' said Callum. 'I can ring either one of them now if you want. Dwight's probably best because he was the one who took the plates in the first place.'

Dwight walked aimlessly along the waterfront of Battery Park, people watching and looking out over the Hudson River glinting benignly in the autumn sunshine. Things around him registered, yet there was that enduring numbness, a feeling of unreality somehow. It was like he was watching himself in a movie; one about a successful guy who had it all and fell to pieces because he always wanted more.

As his mind seemed to tune in and out, as if filled with static from a cheap radio, Dwight eventually realised his phone was playing his call tune. He still didn't want to speak to anyone, but wondered who was calling nonetheless and looked at the number. Even through the mental fog, he remembered the UK dialling code, but couldn't think beyond the idea of a scam call. So, he switched the phone off, replacing it in the bag with a dead, black screen.

Remi had rung the bell, rapped hard on the door and waited several minutes outside Dwight's apartment until he was convinced he wasn't in. Or was it more serious than that, given the fact he wasn't answering his phone either? What was he to do now? How could he possibly find a man in a city of millions if he wasn't home and couldn't be contacted? Just as Remi was turning disconsolately back towards the elevator, unsure what to do next, his phone rang. It wasn't a number he recognised, but he answered anyway.

'Hello.'

'Hiya. Is that Remi?'

'Yep.'

'It's Callum Craigie from Orkney. I took you to the *Vanguard* last week.'

'Oh. Er, hi, Callum,' said Remi, aware of a chugging sound, as if the caller was on a boat.

'Do you know where Dwight is?'

'I sure wish I did. I'm just outside his apartment but there's no one here. He's not answering his phone either.'

'Aye, I know. I've just tried ringing him and couldn't get through.'

'Well, that makes two of us. What can I do for you, Callum?'

'It's a bit complicated. I'll put Laura on. Do y' remember her from The Murray Arms? She'll explain.' The phone went silent for a few seconds, then Remi heard a young woman's voice.

'Hello, Remi.'

'Hi.'

'I don't think we spoke, but I remember you were in the restaurant after your diving.'

'Yeah, that was me, and big Dwight, of course,' laughed Remi awkwardly, not knowing where the conversation was heading.

'Do you remember the plates you, er, found at the *Vanguard* wreck site?'

'Yeah,' replied Remi with a mixture of caution and intrigue.

'I know this'll sound weird, but there's been some, er, strange goings-on, which all seem linked to the mess plates.'

'Strange stuff? Like what exactly?'

'Well, believe it or not, ghosts of sailors, wet footprints with no explanation, damage to property, possibly even a drowning – lots of things that have all seemed to follow the plates around. A few of us have experienced it. It's all been… well, pretty bizarre and scary to be honest.'

Remi's mouth set in a tight, worrisome line. It was as if a growing itch had finally been scratched and he was beginning to understand.

'Are things OK now though?' asked Remi.

'Sort of. We've got the support of some priests and, er, a medium.'

After a pause, 'Wow,' was all Remi could offer.

'Do you know where the third plate is, Remi?'

'Dwight has it, or at least had it. I'm actually looking for him in New York having flown in from Boston earlier because I was worried about him. Since being on Orkney, he seems to have gone off the rails and now he isn't answering his phone. It's really concerning.'

'You're right to be worried, judging by what's happened here. You really need to find him, and probably a priest as well.'

'Right,' said Remi grimly. 'I'll do my best, though it's a long shot in New York.'

'And if you find the plate, please contact us because we need it back here as soon as possible.'

'What? You're three thousand miles away!'

'I know. But we don't think this thing will be over until the plates are back on the *Vanguard*.'

Though Remi hadn't taken the plates, at that moment he felt ashamed. He'd been party to the theft, after all.

'I'll do my best, and sorry to hear about the trouble over there. I'll let you know how I get on.'

'That's great, Remi. Thank you. Bye.'

'Bye,' said Remi, before letting out a deep sigh and wondering where to go in his search for what seemed like a tiny needle in a field of haystacks.

Dwight walked along the tree-lined water's edge looking out absently towards Ellis Island and the Statue of Liberty. His thoughts were random, disconnected, without clear meaning, while feelings seemed to bubble inside like a simmering stew of emotions. As he looked at the ferry ploughing a watery furrow towards the nearby terminal, the plate in the rucksack seemed to dig into his back and he felt a desperate urge to be rid of it.

In response, Dwight walked briskly off the path to the very edge of the water, removed the plate from the rucksack and held it up like the quarterback he once was, ready to throw it as far into the Hudson River as he could. As he tensed to release it, he spotted a dark shadow in the water only a few yards from the lapping shore. Dwight lowered the plate and stared into the shallows, before gasping in anguish as he discerned what the shape was.

Swimming breaststroke beneath the surface and moving towards him was a sailor, his navy uniform billowing with each stroke. As he came closer, his head tilted upwards and Dwight recognised the accusing eyes that bore into him once more. In that desperate moment, Dwight could think of only one way to stop him and he wasn't going to hesitate.

Once Remi was back on the street, his stomach rumbled and he looked at his watch. It was just after twelve and he hadn't eaten since having a cookie on the flight nearly three hours ago. That decided his next move: find something to eat, then work out what to do next before he flew back later that evening.

The shade of the tall apartment block and the surrounding buildings persuaded Remi to head for the waterfront and the sunshine, where it would also be a little quieter than the hectic Manhattan streets. He picked up his pace in search of an eatery and headed beyond the One World Trade Center, where there was a choice of restaurants. He soon found a vacant table outside an Italian and was promptly passed a menu by a smiling waitress. *If he was on what looked increasingly like a fool's errand, he may as well enjoy a good lunch and – what the hell? – have a glass of wine too. He might think better if he relaxed a little.*

Remi enjoyed his risotto and white wine before digging into a large piece of tiramisu, though thoughts of Dwight still sat heavily on him. He'd also drawn a blank on any fresh ideas as to how he might find him, while phoning and texting yet again proved fruitless. Short of wandering the streets looking for one face among potentially millions, he could think of no other way of tracing him. If he went to the police all he could think they'd do is take some details. And even if they knew something, they wouldn't tell Remi because he was only a friend.

Remi concluded that further searching was futile. With another six hours until his flight, he decided to have a walk along the shoreline to liven up after his heavy lunch, then try Dwight's apartment again before heading back to JFK.

Stepping briskly away from the restaurant, Remi looked to cross North End Avenue but had to halt abruptly on the kerb as a police car sped past with sirens screaming and blue lights flashing, followed closely by an ambulance. He walked towards the waterfront, stopping for a few minutes to survey the small green pasture and stone skeleton of a farm dwelling atop the Irish Hunger Memorial, incongruous yet striking amid Manhattan's towering glass and concrete. Close behind it lay the lawns and tree-fringed shoreline and, as Remi moved beyond the memorial, his thoughts turned from the horrors of the Irish Potato Famine to the speeding police car and ambulance that were now parked just ahead, joining another police vehicle already on the scene.

Remi spotted activity in the trees as he walked closer. Police were cordoning an area off by the water as the ambulance crew wheeled a gurney towards the yellow-taped area. They moved slowly, a sign their role had changed. They probably weren't there to treat a patient anymore, but to collect a body.

Remi usually avoided such scenes, yet inexplicably he was drawn forwards. As the bed of the gurney was lowered, then pushed through the taped cordon, Remi walked faster. He could see a young female cop holding an orange Nike rucksack. Remembering that Dwight had one like it, Remi's heart quickened as his pace dropped.

Adrenaline coursing through him, Remi kept walking towards the scene. The cop shouted at him as he reached the yellow tape.

'Hey! This is off limits just now!'

'Yeah, I can see, but I think I recognise that bag.'

'What?' said the cop incredulously. 'Why'd you say that?'

Remi exhaled sadly. 'Because my friend had one like it and he lives nearby.'

As the cop walked towards him, Remi noticed movement over her shoulder. The gurney had now been loaded and was right behind her, the crew stopping to zip the corpse into a black body bag.

‘Oh, God,’ said Remi quietly on seeing the familiar blond hair soaked and plastered to the forehead. ‘I know that guy.’

‘You do? Who do you think it is, sir?’ asked the cop, her tone softer now.

‘Dwight O’Neil,’ said Remi, suddenly light-headed.

Her face was grave as she beckoned her sergeant over.

23

The bar of The Murray Arms was a welcoming place to be after a wet, frightening episode on Scapa Flow earlier that day. All who had been aboard the *Peedie Star*, apart from Gary Bremner, were there. Gary was at home after a hospital visit had confirmed he had mild concussion, while the rest of the group met to consider what to do next.

Once all were settled with a drink, Alan Muir took the lead.

'Has anyone had any more thoughts on what we should do now?' he asked, looking round the table.

'I've had a lot of thoughts,' said Shona, 'but what I think we should do still hasn't changed.'

'Same here. I've kicked it around and prayed on it, and I still think getting the third plate back is our best option,' said Helen.

'Let's face it. We could have lost Callum today – for the second time in a week! I don't think we can risk another trip to the *Vanguard* without that other plate,' added Jean. Her words were met by grave nods.

'An' if we get the third plate back,' said Callum, 'as the guy said in Jaws, "We're gonna need a bigger boat!"' This prompted a chorus of laughter that died quickly when Callum's phone rang on the table.

'Hello?'

'Hi. Is that Callum?' asked Remi.

'Aye. It's Remi, isn't it?' replied Callum as he identified the accent and put the phone into speaker mode.

'It is. Er, this isn't easy but I may as well get straight to it. Dwight's dead.'

'What? How?'

The whole group sat in silence, exchanging worried glances.

'I don't know yet. He was pulled out of the Hudson River earlier this afternoon. I'm not long out the police station. I guess me showing up at the point they found him seemed suspicious, me knowing him and all.' Remi sounded exhausted. Flat.

'Are you OK? Is there anyone else with you?' asked Helen eventually. 'Oh, I'm Helen, by the way. There's a group of us here, Remi, who are all involved. You're on speaker if that's OK.'

'Yeah, no problem. I'm pretty shocked but I'm OK. Oh, the other thing is, I've got the plate.'

'Really?' said Laura, as the other five instinctively leant forward, listening intently.

'It's weird, but after the police let me go, I came back to where Dwight was found. Near the taped-off area on the shoreline, I saw the plate in some long grass. The cop standing guard was looking the other way, so, knowing you guys want it, I slipped it in my rucksack.'

There was a range of expressions around the table at the surprising news. Both Helen and Jean's mouths dropped open. Shona and Callum smiled, while Alan raised his eyebrows. Laura frowned before speaking again.

'That's really brilliant news. How soon could you get it here?' she asked.

'Well, I guess I could post it right away. I don't want to hang on to it, that's for sure,' said Remi. On hearing this, Shona shook her head violently.

'But it might break!' she said loudly. 'Who knows what will come about if that happens!'

Jean and Callum nodded, as did Laura.

'Can't you bring it over?' asked Shona. 'Oh, I'm Shona by the way.'

'Er… well, Shona, I'd, er, like to, but my boss isn't happy about me taking today off, never mind more days. And, well, I can't afford the flight either.'

'How much is it?' asked Callum.

'About a thousand dollars I guess, including the flight from Edinburgh to Kirkwall. That's what I paid last time.'

'I'll pay it,' said Callum, triggering a collection of raised eyebrows, then smiles.

'Hey, that's really kind, man, but I'm not sure it's that simple. I've got work, family…'

'Hello, Remi. This is Alan Muir here, I'm a local priest.

We can all see it's not easy for you to just jump on a plane, but we wouldn't ask if wasn't so important. We've had a death and injuries here linked to these plates and there's possibly another one in Dwight. All we ask is that you try your best to come as soon as you can.'

There was a short silence as Remi seemed to be weighing Alan's words.

'OK. I'll do my best, but I'm finding this whole thing… Dwight… the plates… problems over with you guys… it's just hard to get my head around.'

'I can imagine, aye,' said Shona. 'But we've got to deal with this, and quickly!'

'Yeah, I get it. Look, I'll make a few calls and get back to you guys, OK?'

24

Remi looked down the length of the Edinburgh-bound jet from his rear aisle seat, scarcely able to believe he would be returning to Orkney less than a week after he'd left. This time, though, he was on his own and, as that thought registered, the image of Dwight's pale, lifeless face returned once more, as it had so many times since yesterday. It was hard to grasp. A man who was so vital and alive only days ago was now lying inert in a cold fridge, awaiting his final journey to a hole in the ground.

Given Dwight's fate and what he'd heard yesterday from the people on Orkney, Remi was also apprehensive about carrying the plate, currently stowed in the overhead locker. He remembered too how the flight out of Kirkwall had dropped violently after take-off, and he was braced for something similar this time. Thankfully, it hadn't materialised – at least, not yet. He tried to reassure himself that if this medium on Orkney was right and the plate had to be returned, by helping with that return, he'd hopefully be safe. Hopefully…

At least Remi wasn't stressing about work. His boss had been decent when Remi explained about Dwight's death and how he "needed a few days to help sort out some of his affairs". He'd offered Remi leave for Thursday and Friday on the condition that he was back in on Monday, plus a couple of days later for the funeral once the date was confirmed.

Remi also felt fortunate that he wouldn't be out of pocket. It had certainly made for an easier conversation when he told Kim he'd been asked to fly to Orkney and his flights and accommodation were being paid for owing to Callum's generosity, plus Shona wangling two free nights at The Murray Arms because of a late cancellation. Kim had been exasperated at first, but when he explained that two people were now dead – and coupled with her strong belief in the supernatural since a childhood experience – she had soon come round.

Yet Remi remained troubled. How could he not be after Dwight's death and all that he'd heard about events on Orkney? Talk of him finding a priest concerned him too, especially as he was an atheist. He also didn't know how he felt about being asked to return to *HMS Vanguard* with the plates. It seemed only fitting, but would he find the spot on the wreck site again where the plates had been found? And who would his dive partner be? It was a deep dive, after all. As Remi looked down on a serene expanse of fluffy cloud, his mind continued to whirl anxiously.

While Remi cruised high above the Atlantic, Laura Matson was holding the rail of the Houton to Lyness ferry as it battled through a heavy swell. She was focusing on the horizon, hoping desperately not to see her lunch make a reappearance as cold spray spattered over the deck once more. It wasn't as rough as it had been yesterday on the *Peedie Star*, but that had only been for a few minutes. This wallowing, rocking journey had lasted for nearly half an hour, though was thankfully almost over. The dock was close now and the sea beginning to settle.

Laura reflected on how she'd become part of a group in recent days, bound together by their involvement in a bizarre series of events. What had happened still seemed unreal, though she knew it to be frighteningly true. Yet she was less scared now than she'd been the previous Friday, supposedly alone at home, though not completely, as the wet footprints and the opening of doors by themselves had revealed. Fortunately, Shona, Alan and Helen had all helped, firstly by believing her, then in providing some reassurance, and especially by blessing her house. It was strange to think how she'd welcomed and wanted the blessing, yet a week ago would have thought it weird and irrelevant. She'd also met David Innes, the first man Laura had given more than a second thought to since moving to Orkney, and she was certainly looking forward to seeing him again today.

Alan sat on the damp deck seat looking ahead towards the Lyness Dock, huddled into his waterproof, while Helen stood excitedly at the rail, clearly unfazed by the choppy waters.

'This is another place I've wanted to visit for a long time. I used to teach about the scuttling of the German fleet in Scapa Flow – the biggest mass sinking in maritime history!' enthused Helen loudly as she turned towards him. Alan nodded and smiled.

'I'm sure they'll let you have a look round the museum once you've done the blessing,' he replied.

'I hope so! There's got to be some perks to this work!' laughed Helen.

As with Laura, Alan's world was also a lot different to that of a week ago. He'd been shocked and shaken out of a despondent and destructive rut, and his faith had returned. Indeed, praying in silence next to Helen Hughes this morning in the empty kirk where the mess plates sat, thankfully inert, on the altar, was like being suddenly reconnected to a spiritual dimension. A room within, a space of peace and power, closed off from him for so long had opened once more.

Yet Alan knew this wasn't just about the hauntings. It was also about Helen Hughes. To her, following God was less about rules and more about how you treated others. In short, Helen was an antidote to the pious religiosity of so many churches, often now as empty as the mumbled hymns and absently recited prayers. Yet she didn't pretend to have all the answers. Helen knew this world, and everything beyond it, was infinitely complex and approached that mystery in a simple yet profound way. To Alan, she was the brightest window on God he'd ever seen. Someone who loved cake as much as prayer and a hearty laugh as much as peaceful silence. For Alan, Helen also brought something else: hope. A daring hope that she might yet remain in his life for longer than a few more days.

David Innes looked at his watch for the fifth time in ten minutes and it didn't escape Katie's attention.

'She won't get here any faster if you look at your watch, y'know! Besides, the ferry's just docked so you need to check your hair's OK, quick!' chided Katie.

David gave a weak smile and resisted the urge to run his hand over his hair.

'Come on, Katie. This is serious business this afternoon,' said David.

Closing the museum for an hour had not been well received by a few customers, particularly those who wanted to use the café – though the offer of free coffee and cake later had appeased most. Yet David remained a mixture of apprehension and frustration as they waited for Helen Hughes to arrive in order to conduct the blessing.

Katie spotted Laura, accompanied by Alan and Helen, crossing the concourse, noting how Helen was animatedly pointing at the massive propeller and drive shaft of *HMS Hampshire.*

'Looks like the vicar likes her history,' said Katie, as she moved to the door to welcome them. 'Still all feels weird though,' she added, with an involuntary shiver.

'Aye, it does,' said David, joining her at the entrance and breaking into a smile as he spotted Laura striding to the door.

'Hello! Welcome to Scapa Flow Museum!' said Katie as they stepped inside.

'Nice to see you again, Laura,' added David. Laura beamed at him and Katie noticed a hint of flushing at her throat.

With the introductions over, the five of them went into the office, where Helen asked David to recount what had happened at the museum over a coffee and biscuits. While she'd already heard the story from Laura, who she trusted, Helen felt the need to see if there was anything additional and possibly significant in what David said himself. She also knew that listening established a bond and helped people relax in a situation they found strange, particularly if they weren't used to priests. By the time David had finished, aided by Katie, Helen had donned her purple stole and was holding her bottle of holy water.

'I've also brought a spare in case I run out, given that it's a big place,' said Helen with a grin, indicating she had a second bottle in her large handbag. 'So, without further ado, let's make a start!'

At that, David began guiding Helen through the museum, while Laura, Alan and Katie followed behind, serious and mute as Helen's prayers sounded around the high-roofed spaces brimming with stories and objects from the past. In the *HMS Vanguard* section, David removed the tarpaulin from the cabinet and was relieved to see through the pock-marked glass that the objects had not moved since Katie had returned them to their original positions.

As they moved through the galleries, the prayers repeated and the holy water splashed, David didn't know how he felt about it and neither did Katie. That said, given what had happened with the footprints and the cabinet, neither thought it wasn't worth doing, even if it seemed a little odd.

Once the whole interior had been blessed, they returned to the office, where Katie kindly busied herself once again making drinks and Helen talked animatedly about the museum and beamed when David said she was welcome to have a look around. Over a second coffee, David asked about yesterday's aborted trip and they explained the new plan of waiting for the third plate to arrive back in Orkney.

'Only then, when all three plates are back on the ship, do we think there'll be closure on this matter,' said Alan.

'That's our hope anyway,' added Laura.

'So, you're going back in the small boat – which sounds like it nearly sank yesterday – but banking on better weather because you'll have all the plates?' asked David dubiously.

'We're using a different boat, a bigger one, called the *Blue Raven*,' replied Alan Muir.

'Oh aye. I know it. It's a proper dive boat,' said David. 'How did you get that at short notice?'

'Contacts,' said Laura, tapping her nose and grinning. 'Callum, the guy that took the Americans out to the wreck, works on the dive boats and he's sorted it for us.'

'Can't have been cheap. I've dived from the *Blue Raven* myself,' said David.

'You dive?' asked Alan.

'Oh, aye. I've been diving on the German wrecks for a few years now. Working here got me interested.'

'How do you feel about diving to the *Vanguard* tomorrow?' added Laura.

'Me? Well… it's a protected war grave, for a start,' stammered David.

'But you'll be returning the mess plates,' said Laura.

'Without official permission, I take it?' he asked.

Alan nodded, then spoke gravely. 'Setting up something official will take time and we need to act fast to prevent further harm.'

'If I'm found out, it's not a good look for the Scapa Flow Museum manager, is it?'

'It looks like you'd be doing the right thing to me,' said Laura. David's pursed lips showed he was now seriously considering it.

'Who else is in the dive team?' asked David.

'One of the Americans who's bringing the plate back. He's been to the wreck before too,' offered Laura.

'Why's only one of them coming?'

Laura, Alan and Helen all looked at each other before Helen grasped the nettle.

'One of them died yesterday. We don't yet know how,' she said quietly.

David's eyes widened before Katie interjected.

'Come on, David Innes! You're Hoy's resident action man! If you're found out righting a wrong diving to one of the ships this museum's dedicated to, it'll only enhance your reputation. And besides, if you die, there's an excellent deputy ready to step in to the breach!'

David laughed, but it wasn't Katie's words swaying him; Laura's beseeching blue eyes were what he couldn't say no to.

'Do you know if this American guy's PADI-trained for deeper dives?'

'I'm sure he will be,' said Laura. 'Callum said they've travelled all over the world wreck diving, and had been out with Scapa Adventures earlier in the week.'

'He must be qualified then,' said David with a nod. 'Scapa Adventures want to see proof you can dive to the depths you're aiming to go down to.'

'So?' asked Laura with a wide-eyed look. David crumbled.

'OK. What time do we depart and where from?' he asked with a smile.

'It's a three o' clock sailing to give Remi – the American guy – a little more time to be ready after his flight. And the *Blue Raven* is in Stromness,' said Alan.

'OK. I'll get my gear ready after work and head to mainland tonight. As Katie said, I've got a brilliant deputy to step into the breach.'

'Where will you stay?' asked Laura.

'My brother's on mainland,' said David.

'It's just that if you wanted, you could stay with me,' said Laura. 'In my spare room, that is.' The words seemed to be out before she'd really thought about them. Then she coloured up at the thought of how her offer might be construed, especially by two priests. Yet Alan was simply impassive, while Helen smiled as broadly as Katie.

'Oh, OK. That's kind of you, Laura,' said David, with a hint of crimson showing above his beard.

Remi had tried to savour the merlot he'd drunk but he was just too on edge. Then an odd, panicky thought came to him. *Was the plate safe? Of course it is,* he told himself. He'd checked his rucksack before the departure gate and had even touched the bubble wrap it was cocooned in. *But what if it had been stolen in the airport and only the bubble wrap had been left? How could it be stolen when he had it the whole time? But it was on his back. A thief could have removed it when he queued for that coffee. But it was highly, highly unlikely, and besides, the bag had felt quite heavy when he'd lifted it into the overhead locker. Were thieves now carrying round weights to place in people's bags so they wouldn't know anything had been taken? As if.*

Remi knew this dialogue with himself was crazy. The plate was there. *It was just that… Besides, the two seats next to him were empty, so he could easily take a quick look to get this overwrought monkey off his back.*

So, he gave in to his sudden neurosis, stood up, opened the overhead locker and reached the blue rucksack down with such care it looked as if he was handling either a priceless vase or an unstable bomb. Remi sat down again and placed the bag on the adjacent seat, opening it carefully. He took a deep, relieved breath as he felt the plate through the bubble wrap, though he opened it up just to be doubly sure. The plate felt cold, uncomfortable somehow.

'Must be valuable, huh?'

Remi looked across the aisle at a young, whippet-thin man with sharp features and searching, greedy eyes. The blue suit and Rolex marked him down as a business flyer, though his seat in standard suggested he was still very much climbing the ladder.

Remi smiled. 'Not really, just sentimental value.'

'What is it?' asked the man.

'It's a mess plate from a British warship, something the sailors would eat off.'

'How'd you get it?'

'Er, a friend found it.'

'What, in the sea?'

'Yeah,' said Remi, keen to end the conversation, but Rolex was just warming up. He moved quickly across the aisle and perched on the outer seat in Remi's row, thrusting his hand out and grabbing at the plate. Remi resisted momentarily, but then let the guy handle it rather than cause offence. Rolex turned the plate over in his hands, appraising it.

'How much d'ya want for it?'

'Sorry, it's not for sale,' smiled Remi awkwardly, heat spreading across his neck.

'You know what they say – everything has a price, right?' said Rolex.

'Not this,' said Remi, serious now in tone and expression, his right hand held out expectantly.

Rolex passed the plate back, his face stoney, before standing. As he turned his back on Remi, he muttered, 'Strange guy.'

No sooner had he spoken than the aircraft dropped suddenly, sending Rolex sprawling over the female passenger seated next to him. She screamed in shock as his left hand found her breast. Meanwhile, other voices of alarm filled the plane as it continued to judder like an old truck bouncing along a rutted road.

Remi gripped on to the plate and, despite the vibration, slotted it back into the bubble wrap then into the rucksack, before hugging it close to him. As soon as he did so, the turbulence stopped, though his heart kept up a rapid, chest-banging beat for several minutes.

The disembodied voice of the pilot echoed round the cockpit. 'Sorry for the unexpected turbulence we just experienced, folks. We'll keep the "seatbelt fastened" signs on for now and ask you to remain seated. Trolley service and use of the restrooms will hopefully resume shortly. Thank you.'

Remi stole a look at Rolex, who was turned away from his neighbour in embarrassment, his head hanging, his eyes seemingly finding the aisle carpet of great interest. It sounded the bell for another round of Remi-style wrangling, though there was a lighter side to his musings on the supernatural. *If ghosts exist, could they really have a sense of humour?* Remi wondered.

25

Remi sat forward stiffly, changing position on the hard wire chair close to the departure gate for his evening flight to Orkney. He'd arrived from Boston in the late afternoon after just under seven hours in the air and would soon spend another hour back in the sky, his fourth flight in two days. The travelling, the shock of Dwight's death and the impending dive with what seemed to be a cursed plate could be seen in Remi's furrowed brow, which knitted deep lines above tired eyes.

His phone pinged and he smiled at the message from Kim.

> Hi, baby. Great to hear you made it to Edinburgh in time for the Orkney flight.
>
> All good here. Holly sends hugs. How about a call later? Kx

The man sat to his right heard the ping and looked over Remi's shoulder to read the message. *Either this guy cradling his phone with a sickly smile was one of the few lucky men to have a great partner or he was just another sucker being lied to. For all Smiler knows, she may well have some guy in all night,* mused Matthew Stone.

Matthew Stone had endured a long day, having driven up to Edinburgh from York. He'd moved there from London last year after a difficult break-up from a woman who just seemed to change overnight and ran out on him. *Sure, he was big enough to admit he could be a bit harsh, particularly when stressed with work, something she never seemed to understand. And yes, he'd gone over the top a couple of times and lashed out. But he'd never meant to hurt her. There was no real force used, yet however much he apologised, she wasn't having it, then upped and left.*

He'd tried to track her down a few times. He even went to the school where she worked, but they just closed ranks and wouldn't tell him anything, fobbing him off with some GDPR bollocks. It was like she'd disappeared off the face of the Earth.

So, he moved on and got a tasty promotion to a firm in York, where he had a nice flat and a couple of willing women on the go. Nothing heavy, just friends with benefits – much better and less stress than living with a neurotic bitch where he was constantly minding his Ps and Qs and making sure he'd put the toilet seat back down, for God's sake.

Then fate played a hand and he thought he might have found her, all because of a bloody painting. A work mate had invited him round to watch football and he saw this picture on the table that he'd bought on holiday, ready to hang in his bathroom. It was a seascape in watercolour, somewhere in Orkney apparently. But it wasn't really the picture that caught his eye; it was the artist's signature. Or rather, the simple initial. It was an italicised L. He knew someone who wrote Ls just like that: his former partner, Laura Matson.

The guy said he'd bought the picture in a town called Kirkwall, in a little shop on the main street. When he looked online, it seemed to be a half-arsed little place. How hard could it be to find a small shop flogging paintings? He figured that if he found the shop, he could hopefully trace the artist, then spring a surprise. Not that he wanted to hurt her. Oh no, he could just see her running to the cops for some restraining order or something. He just wanted her to know he was doing well without her, thank you very much. And that, despite her best efforts to hide, he'd still found her in the end. He could just see her face.

Laura and Callum sat in Kirkwall Airport nursing takeaway coffees, looking expectantly in the direction of the arrivals door where Remi Binks should appear at any moment. David, meanwhile, was in the toilet. They'd heard the whine of the turboprops a few minutes before and knew from experience that it didn't take long to empty such a small aircraft and for people to claim their baggage.

As the doors opened and the first passengers stepped through, Laura and Callum searched the faces, looking for the small, dark-haired American. Then Laura stopped searching and focused on one particular face that caused her stomach to lurch. Walking briskly in her direction was her former partner, Matthew Stone.

Matthew was collecting a hire car and as he gazed around, searching for the kiosk, he spotted Laura. She was already looking at him, her mouth open and eyes wide. It was definitely her. She hadn't changed at all. He masked his surprise and stared back, unblinking, affecting a grin. He strode ever closer, dragging a small-wheeled case in the wake of a long, cream overcoat and matching suede boots.

'Well, hello, Laura!' he announced.

'Hello, Matthew,' she replied quietly, eyes downcast, heart thumping. Callum sensed her discomfort and watched closely.

'So, you ran away to the Orkneys. No wonder I couldn't find you,' he said lightly, keeping the smile in place.

'Why are you here, Matthew?' said Laura sharply, suddenly looking up at him. Callum frowned and shifted in his seat.

'Come on, Laura. No need for the attitude, eh.'

'There's every need!' Laura spat, just as David was walking back to where she was seated.

He quickly surmised from the tension in Laura's voice that there was an issue with this man who had struck a dominant pose, close to and above her.

'Is everything OK, Laura?' asked David.

'Everything's fine,' interjected Matthew with a smile, prompting Callum to jump up.

'He's no' askin' you! He's askin' Laura!' snapped Callum, thrusting his finger in Matthew's face.

'And who are you? The ape man of Orkney?' sneered Matthew, at which Callum grabbed him by the lapels and swung him sideways, causing his case to topple over.

'Twat!' shouted Matthew as he struggled with Callum, while David moved smartly behind them, gripped Matthew's right arm and began pushing him forcefully towards the door.

'My case!'

'I'll get it for you once we've had a word outside,' said David evenly, smiling at a few astonished bystanders witnessing the ruckus as Matthew was manhandled to the exit. Meanwhile, Laura seemed to shut down. She put her head in her hands, as if she was blocking everything out.

Matthew had stopped struggling by the time he was outside, realising these were two burly and evidently strong characters, the younger of which looked like he'd been in a recent fight, with his swollen mouth and scarred nose. To his relief, they took their hands off him once they were through the doors, but they were still uncomfortably close.

'OK then, pal, what's the story with Laura?' asked David with a flinty glare, Callum at his side.

'I don't know what you mean.'

'She's clearly upset by you. Why?' persisted David, his question accompanied this time by a hard poke in the chest.

'We used to be an item. We lived together in London,' said Matthew, shoulders slumped now. 'And I swear to God, I just walked into the airport and saw her there. I didn't know she was here, really.'

'So why come to Orkney?'

'Just a short break.'

'So, what've you come to see? Because you're hardly here for the weather,' demanded David.

'Er… Kirkwall. I'm staying there for three nights, just having a look round.'

'What at exactly?' asked David.

'Just a general look round, y'know,' said Matthew, aware it sounded weak even before David and Callum curled their lips in ridicule.

'Callum, get this guy's bag, please. He's just going,' said David, before leaning so close to Matthew he could smell his breath. 'I'm giving you the benefit of the doubt. But it's clear Laura doesn't want to see you. So if you see her again, walk the other way, because if you don't, I'll want to know why and I won't be as polite as I am now. D'ye understand?'

Matthew nodded as Callum dropped the case heavily on his foot, marking his boots and causing him to flinch.

'Four words,' said Callum.

'What?' asked Matthew, still wincing.

'Fuck off and disappear!'

'But I'm collecting a car. I need to go back inside,' said Matthew.

'OK. But we're watching you,' warned David.

At that, Matthew limped back inside, studiously avoiding looking towards Laura and feeling four angry Orcadian eyes burning into his back.

Remi had been stopped by a female customs official, who carefully emptied his bag and took a particular interest in the mess plate after getting him to remove all the bubble wrap. When he was asked what it was, Remi explained that it was a naval mess plate he'd brought for Alan Muir, a local priest who had two others that were the same. The woman smiled at the mention of Alan's name and helped Remi re-pack, before wishing him a pleasant time diving, having seen his diving mask and gloves.

It had just been a random check, but Remi asked himself whether he looked suspicious as he dragged his case through the doors and looked for Callum. He quickly spotted his red hair and stocky frame, though was shocked to see the damage to his face, then remembered being told about the accident. He recognised Laura too from The Murray Arms, though she seemed to be with another guy, who had his arm protectively round her shoulder. She also looked ashen, scared even. *What had he got into by returning to Orkney?*

Once greetings, introductions and condolences regarding Dwight had been made, they walked to Laura's car, where David joined her in the front and Remi ducked into the rear with Callum. They took an agreed detour into Kirkwall as David punched Alan Muir's number in his phone to let him know that Remi had landed and they were on their way to the kirk. Remi heard Alan say he would set off from home immediately and meet them shortly.

At the kirk, Remi was introduced to Alan and Helen, who he'd only known as disembodied voices at the other end of a phone. While he wasn't a religious man, he liked them immediately. Both seemed warm and sincere, which somehow made him feel a little less anxious.

The kirk was bright under the lights, though cold. In fact, Remi was surprised he couldn't see the mist of their breath as they made their way to the altar. Alan took the mess plate from him, unwrapped it and placed it next to the other two. Then he sat in the front pew next to Helen and prayed openly. David, Callum, Laura and Remi stood behind, watching on quietly. Callum even took off his cap.

'Almighty God, we ask that you bless us as we seek to do your will by returning these plates to their rightful home. Protect us in carrying out our endeavours tomorrow. In the name of Jesus Christ, our Lord. Amen.'

'Amen,' chorused David, Laura and Remi in unison, quickly followed by Callum, who made it sound like an echo. Though none of the four would normally have prayed, at that moment, it just felt right.

26

Helen Hughes woke at dawn. It had been a fitful night of sleep, interspersed with periods of worry that her prayers had failed to dispel. She propped herself up on one elbow and pulled the curtain aside to reveal a mackerel sky. The forecast for rain late morning, followed by dry weather, looked as if it might well be correct and augured well for their trip to *HMS Vanguard* in the afternoon.

As she pulled herself into a sitting position on the bed with a sigh, she put her hands together to give thanks for the day ahead and began to pray, committing whatever lay ahead to God. When she rose to shower after a few minutes, she felt more peaceful and positive. It led her to wonder once more why things often seemed so different in the morning compared to the darkness, both physical and mental, that sometimes descended in the early hours.

Alan smiled to himself in bed as he heard Helen shuffling along the hall to the bathroom. Though he'd felt a jolt of adrenaline after waking when he remembered what lay in store that Friday, overall, he felt quite composed after a good night's sleep. He'd enjoyed another night in Helen's company and was thankful they'd gone through a few days now without anything untoward happening that could be attributed to the plates. Yet Alan remained wary. He was keen to see the plates returned to the ship as soon as possible and hoped that a line would be drawn under what had been quite possibly the most bizarre episode in his life.

It had not all been bad, though. Confronted by the reality of things beyond his ken, Alan's faith had returned. He'd also stopped his destructive drinking, which, after the first few difficult nights, hadn't been an issue simply because each evening he'd had the one thing he most needed: company. Though not just company – Helen's enjoyable, stimulating presence had lifted him so much. So, while Alan was hoping this afternoon's trip would result in a definitive end to the supernatural events, he also knew that would mean Helen returning to Carlisle. In truth, he wanted her to stay.

Laura was already dressed and seated at the breakfast table, eating her Corn Flakes by seven a.m. She could hear the shower in the adjacent room, indicating that David was now out of bed. It was a reassuring sound, that of company, and although there'd been no more ghostly happenings after the previous Friday night, she would have been lying if she'd said she hadn't thought about it each time she'd retired to bed since.

What had been equally shocking, though, had been the sight of Matthew at the airport. She'd woken a few times in the night recalling what had happened with a sense of incredulity and a few waves of panic, thankfully tempered by hearing David's reassuring rhythmic snore from her guest room. He'd been so kind the night before, listening to her talk about her time with Matthew and her escape from London. He was the first person she'd spoken to about it since moving to Orkney and she felt a sense of relief, though couldn't really explain why.

She'd voiced the fact that she sometimes wondered if hiding from Matthew had been the right thing. David had responded by saying that after last night, there was no more wondering, adding that Matthew might now know where Laura was, but also that she had some solid friends. As she'd looked across at David's broad frame and brawny arms, she mused with a smile that "solid" was a good word to use. And yes, she'd been shaken, but she was also angry, as much with herself as Matthew, for allowing him to still have some grip on her life. From now on she would fight it, starting with dismissing any more thoughts of moving again. She loved Orkney. It was her home and she'd be damned if she'd lose her friends, her lifestyle and the beauty that surrounded her every day because of a half-man she'd once been foolish enough to live with.

She was also enjoying David's company. She wanted more and hoped he felt the same. They'd talked late into the night, swapping backstories. Laura had heard how he'd returned to Hoy after doing his degree in London and working at the Maritime Museum in Greenwich, and they realised with a laugh that they'd lived in the capital at the same time.

Eventually, with eyes drooping, they'd peeled themselves from the sofa and shuffled from the lounge. David had been the perfect gentleman and gone to the spare bedroom, though the slight awkwardness from both when they reached the hall revealed an undeniable subtext. It was certainly one Laura hoped to decipher at some stage, though she couldn't yet say when. Whatever this evening would bring, she was certainly looking forward to spending it with David.

Yet tonight seemed a lifetime away. They had the trip to the *Vanguard* to navigate first and after their turbulent earlier trip on the *Peedie Star*, Laura, like everyone else, had some apprehension about this afternoon's trip on the *Blue Raven*.

Remi had woken feeling wired yet fatigued at the same time. It wasn't a surprise in the light of all that had occurred that week and given what was to come. As he looked around the room it felt surreal to Remi that he was back at The Murray Arms less than seven days since he'd left. In that time, Dwight had died and there'd been apparent mayhem on Orkney too, supposedly unleashed by the plates being raised from the *Vanguard*. Then there was the weird turbulence on the plane a second time. Heck, it was like something out of a horror film.

While Remi couldn't fathom what was going on, he

did know that terrible things had happened to Dwight and several others, and it needed to stop. So, he simply had to go with what was planned and do his bit to help, even if he didn't understand it.

That 'bit' involved a deep dive to an eerie war grave with a new dive partner. Having met David Innes the previous night, his first impressions were of a strong character who thankfully, as a diver, knew the waters of Scapa Flow. The weather forecast was also good for the afternoon. Yet this was Orkney, leading Remi to shudder when he remembered how they'd been suddenly tossed around like a cork on the *Peedie Star* to the point that water was spraying over the sides. Hopefully, this dive boat, the *Blue Raven*, was as solid as Callum had said.

The wound on Callum's nose stung in the cold morning air as he watched Lady running among the bare concrete ruins of the Hoxa Gun battery, her belly low to the coarse grass. What was now a playground for the young collie had once been a complex of buildings, bristling with guns that overlooked waters busy with warships during two world wars. Callum had always enjoyed walking there, looking out across the sound towards the island of Flotta and the hills of Hoy beyond, imagining what it had been like with the soldiers there. He smiled as he spotted the old brick fireplace set in a stone chimney breast, stark against the calm, blue sea, fronted by a rug of grass. The building it had warmed was long gone and the hearth permanently cold, but Callum liked it. What stories had been told as the troops warmed themselves around it on a bitter Orkney evening? What laughter had been heard between men who must have wondered what the future held?

Callum was also thinking about the future, and his immediate fate and that of the others caught up in the events of the last week. He looked at the water and thought back to being under it, as if he was held fast, seemingly waiting to drown. His eyes narrowed at the thought, yet curiously he didn't feel frightened about today, thanks to Auntie Shona. She'd said they'd been given a warning when he'd gone overboard, a signal they needed all the plates back in their rightful place, but all would be well once they were. Given everything that had occurred since Shona first talked about ghostly sailors in The Murray Arms, Callum now simply accepted what she said.

He added up what he'd used out of the money Dwight O'Neil had given him. There'd been one thousand pounds for Gary when they'd used the *Peedie Star*, then another two thousand pounds for the *Blue Raven*, and almost one thousand five hundred pounds for Remi's flights. That left about five hundred pounds, which he intended to use to pay for a meal for everyone going out to the *Vanguard* at Murray's tonight.

Lady ran towards him, tail whipping the air, and he called her name with a joyous shout. It was the call of someone who felt good about himself for once and who'd learnt, to his surprise, that giving could feel a lot better than taking.

27

The *Blue Raven* cut through a slight swell under a heavy sky leaking a cold, stinging rain. The wet weather had arrived later than forecast and the mood aboard was subdued and apprehensive.

Laura was sat on a bench on the rear deck, hood up, hands deep in pockets and mind deep in thought. Close by, David and Remi checked and re-checked equipment, oblivious to the rain mottling their dry suits. Serious eyes and clipped, focused exchanges indicated they too were nervous.

It had been reassuring, though, to hear Remi say he was impressed with the dive boat. Though Laura knew nothing of onboard compressors or dive lifts, it's seventy-foot length and large, heated cabin with room for all eight of them made her feel a lot better about their return to the wreck sight.

Shona joined her and lit up, before considerately holding the cigarette away from her, the smoke curling away on the breeze.

'You OK?' asked Shona, blowing smoke from the side of her mouth.

'Yep. I think so,' replied Laura. 'Seeing David and Remi get geared up to dive all that way down brings it home to you, though.'

'Aye. Diving's a serious business, right enough. But these lads know what they're doing and this is a good operation. I've known Kenny Isbister, the skipper, since I was at school. He'll see us right,' smiled Shona.

'Even if a storm gets up?' said Laura, her mouth a tight line.

'Especially if a storm gets up. The *Blue Raven*'s a different kettle o' fish to the *Peedie Star*. And besides, that hoolan blew up because we didnae have all the plates, but we do now. It'll all be OK.'

Laura nodded. It was what she needed to hear, even if she wasn't entirely convinced.

Helen came out on deck and gave Laura and Shona a broad smile that belied the knot of nerves in her stomach. Her stole lifted on the wind as she moved to the rail and spotted the marker buoy a hundred yards or so ahead. She took a deep breath in and prayed. At first it was just a needed feeling, a sense of something without words, deep calling to deep, as it so often was. Then some words came.

'Lord, help me do your will, not in my own strength, but in yours. Amen.'

'You seemed miles away,' said Alan, joining her on the rail.

'Just getting ready,' said Helen, holding on to her dampening stole before falling silent again, her eyes on the black and yellow buoy that was becoming steadily bigger. The last time she'd seen it, it was swaying like a pendulum.

Remi turned at a rapping on the cabin's window glass, which Kenny Isbister's craggy, bearded features stared through. He grinned widely under his red Aberdeen FC cap and held up an open hand before turning his thumb down.

'Looks like five minutes until we dive,' said Remi, reaching for his fins and mask.

David nodded, then asked, 'Who's carrying the plates?'

'Your call, man. I'm just a tourist.'

There was a thoughtful pause before David answered. 'How about I take them down and you put them in the wreck?'

'I'll go with that,' said Remi, his face taut.

David nodded and forced a smile, adding, 'Looking forward to it!', expressing only a little of what he felt.

Alan approached him, looked at the plates wrapped in the Union flag and produced a small bottle.

'I've some holy water from St Magnus's Cathedral. Shall I bless the plates?'

David shrugged, 'If you like, Alan. Er, thanks.'

'Isn't it all holy water round here?' asked Remi as Alan started to sprinkle the plates, causing him to grin.

The whole party came on to the rear deck, huddled into a collection of rainwear, as Remi and David prepared to dive. Callum walked to the stern, ready to operate the dive lift, swaying easily with the slight swell, as he passed the plates to David in a black rubberised bag.

'Watch yerself, Callum,' said Jean, her words greeted by a tut from her son.

'It's only what I do for a living,' he replied.

'Aye, and the last time you were on a boat you went over the side!' she responded.

Shona touched her sister's arm, 'It'll be OK today, Jean. You'll see.'

Yet all were tense, Shona included, as the lift started to drop, taking Remi and David down, then temporarily out of sight before they swam away from the *Blue Raven*'s hull.

Once in the water, Remi began to focus fully on the dive and the nerves that had sat on his shoulder all day left him. David also zoned in despite a stomach full of butterflies as he cleaned his mask vigorously with spit. Now, they both just wanted to get down there. The others looked on from the stern rail, waving in encouragement as they made a final check of their masks and respirators, signalled to each other with inverted thumbs, then began their descent.

Their dive plan was simple. Drop to fifty feet, find the bow and look for a suitable place to insert the plates safely into the wreck. Remi felt this was a better idea than pushing them back into the seabed somewhere near where Dwight found them. After all, he wasn't even sure he could find the spot again anyway, given there were no obvious reference points.

As they descended into the growing gloom amid a

cascade of bubbles, both Remi and David could feel their hearts thumping and consciously focused on keeping their breathing steady. Fifty feet from the seabed, they levelled off, turned on their torches and looked about them to get a sense of where they were.

Though they had started to descend directly above the bow, they both knew that underwater currents could move them significantly off course and, unsurprisingly, as their torches cut translucent green swathes in the darkness, they could see nothing of the wreck, only the occasional fish glinting in the path of their lights.

Both looked at their dive computers, which indicated they were slightly north of the bow. Remi's gesture to the south was met with an OK from David as they began to kick their fins and search for the wreck.

Remi was strangely uncertain, as if they were groping forwards under a dark, heavy blanket, though he reminded himself he'd felt like this many times before when searching for a wreck. Meanwhile, David simply swam on, engaging one thought: *find the Vanguard, and find her fast.*

Just as Remi's concerns were growing into worry, his torch caught a sharp shape he recognised immediately. The *Vanguard*'s detached bow was directly ahead and below them. David played his beam over it too and a jolt of adrenaline surged within. A ship he knew so much about was suddenly right there, its front section standing solid, separate and sad.

Remi pointed right and they descended slightly and closed on the bow's port side, where an array of starfish clung to its corroding and crusted surface, their orange arms shining in the passing beams. Continuing downwards, almost to the sea floor, they began to see the innards of the ship behind its damaged skin. David marvelled at the thick steel plate bent outwards by the explosion as if it were cardboard.

Remi levelled off before reaching the bottom, careful not to disturb the silt, which would compromise their vision even further, and turned to look inside what had once been part of the officers' quarters on the main deck near the prow of the ship. Through a coffin-sized gap, their torches found some bedframes still showing speckles of white paint under the rust. David shook his head at the sight as he brought the plates out of the bag in their Union flag wrapping, holding them up to Remi as if asking whether they'd found a suitable spot.

Remi took them with an OK and lowered himself forwards to reach into the aperture, looking to place them somewhere secure. He put them down close to the bedframes but as he moved back and shone his torch on them, he thought they might be subject to movement.

He knew that entering the ship was hazardous, but Remi wanted to do this right. So, he flattened himself out and kicked his legs, taking him through the narrow gap. As the space became ever smaller amid the tangled wreckage, Remi recalled his nightmare and couldn't help but look round almost manically for some grasping arms reaching out to grab him.

Come on Remi, stay cool. It was only a dream, he told himself while wedging the plates under some bent metal. Suddenly, pain seared through his left forearm and it immediately felt cold. Then, as he started to back out of the hole, he heard and felt the reverberation of a dull metallic clang. Within a second, everything had gone black.

Laura and Shona stared absently out towards the rising land on Hoy in contemplative silence before Laura looked down at the water.

'They've been down about ten minutes. How long will they be under?' asked Laura.

'About forty minutes tops with one bottle, though I think they're aiming to be in and out in under half an hour.'

'You seem to know a lot about it. Have you done some diving yourself?'

Shona laughed. 'I've done some ducking and diving over the years, but not SCUBA, no. Mind you, you pick up a bit when your hubbie's been a diver.'

'Your Albie was a diver?'

'Oh aye, for near twenty years. He started in the Navy then went on to the oil rigs. Albie's had a bit more excitement than just delivering for Tesco!'

Laura smiled, then frowned. 'I find the whole idea of diving scary, all that water above me.' There was a pause, then she added, 'I just hope they're ok.'

'They'll be fine, I'm sure,' soothed Shona.

'It's just… well, after all that's happened…' said Laura, her words trailing off.

'They'll be up before you know it and you'll have an excuse to give that big guy a lovely hug!' laughed Shona, drawing a coy grin from her younger friend.

While Remi delved into the wreck, David was outside regarding the hull with awe, though after more than a minute had elapsed, he began to wonder what the delay was. He knew that entering a wreck always presented a risk and approached the hole with some concern for his dive partner, just as Remi exited quickly, feet first. Oddly, his fins weren't moving and, once he was clear of the ship, both Remi's arms dropped, blood oozing lazily from the left.

David realised Remi was in trouble and swam towards him, lifting him upright in order to see his face. Remi's eyes were closed, though the bubbles from his respirator showed he was still breathing. David shook him slightly by the shoulders.

Remi felt himself rocking back and forth and could hear his own breath but couldn't see anything.

David was shouting in his head, 'Come on, Remi! Come round, you bugger!'

After twenty seconds, which felt like twenty minutes to David, Remi's eyes opened and he looked slowly about him. His arm was cold and he realised David was holding on to him.

As Remi's thoughts started to align again, he gave the OK sign to David, who promptly removed his hands and let him float. Remi knew where he was and thought he remembered placing the plates in the ship, but he had to be sure.

Remi gestured to David's empty bag and put his finger to his chin as if in thought. The big Scot quickly understood what Remi wanted to know about the plates and knew there was only one way to give a definite answer.

The narrow, jagged gap in the ship was a squeeze for David, but he carefully moved his head and shoulders into the wreck and shone his torch into the space. He smiled inwardly as the beam of light found the plates nestling safely in a small fold in the hull beyond some bedframes.

Remi checked his watch, which showed they'd been underwater for less than sixteen minutes. He'd entered the ship after about fourteen, so must have been unconscious for about sixty seconds. Both men knew that with Remi bleeding and his suit pierced, the sooner they started to ascend the better, given they had decompression stops to complete. So, after a mirror thumbs-up, Remi and David swam away from *HMS Vanguard*, their task completed.

Alan had gathered everyone together on the rail facing the buoy, where they went quiet and looked expectantly at Helen. She smiled broadly as usual and, after making the sign of the cross over the water, raised her head, looked upwards and recited the deliverance prayer.

'Christ within me,
Christ behind me,
Christ before me,
Christ beside me,
Christ to win me,
Christ to comfort and restore me.
Christ beneath me,
Christ in quiet,

Christ in danger,
Christ in hearts of all who love me,
Christ in mouth of friend and stranger.'

After a pause with her eyes closed, Helen nodded at Callum who threw a wreath of poppies on the water, followed by a dozen red roses from Laura as Alan said a short prayer.

'Almighty God, we ask that your presence resides in this place and gives peace to the souls of Scapa Flow. Amen.' There were moist eyes, nods and amens as they watched the vivid flowers spread out on the swirling water. Then the wreath gently touched the buoy and the rain stopped.

Remi and David surfaced within fifty yards of the *Blue Raven*, from which Callum spotted them almost immediately and gave a triumphant shout. David, meanwhile, removed his mask and respirator and swam straight to Remi.

'You OK?' asked David.

'I've been better, but yeah, I think so.'

'What happened in the ship?'

'I must o' banged my head and passed out. It hurts like hell!'

'Your arm's cut too. Come on, let's get back on board.'

'Hey, David. Just to be sure, I got the plates in the ship, right?'

David nodded. 'Yep, nice and snug. I don't know how you floated out though, you were knocked out!'

They then heard excited voices from the *Blue Raven*, where smiling faces appeared above the rail. David and

Remi quickly swam towards the laughter and as they closed in on the boatlift, the sea became calm, the sky clear, and a vivid rainbow arched over Scapa Flow.

28

David and Remi walked into The Murray Arms' restaurant to see the group who'd spent a wet afternoon on the *Blue Raven* now cosily occupying a long table full of drinks, menus and happy chatter.

Callum spotted them first. 'They've let you out, then!' he shouted as everyone turned, grinned and broke into a round of spirited applause that caused David and Remi to take their seats almost bashfully as other diners looked on.

'Y' make it sound like we've been to prison rather than the hospital,' said David with mock indignation once the clapping stopped.

'It felt like a prison when I was in there last week!' replied Callum with a laugh.

'What did they say?' asked Helen.

'Mild concussion and seven stitches,' smiled Remi, holding his bandaged arm up. 'A nice scar to boast about on the dive boats.'

'I got you both a pint of Red McGregor,' said Callum, setting two glasses down as he returned from the bar. 'So, we can now do a toast.'

'A toast?' asked David.

'Aye. To our divers!' said Callum. The phrase echoed happily around the room.

The food appeared, the drink flowed and the conversation and laughter never waned. Remi was enjoying his evening and felt like he was among old friends rather than new acquaintances, though suddenly became tired. His head hurt too and, just as he was starting to feel a little distant and a long way from home, his phone pinged.

He apologised to the group, then looked at the text after seeing it was from Kim.

> Hi, baby. I know it's 8pm where you are, so thought I'd send a message now in case you go to sleep early. I don't understand what's been going on but I know you've done a great thing in helping those folks on Orkney. Holly sends hugs and kisses and so do I. Kx

Remi couldn't help but smile. In a few days he would be home and the hugs and kisses would be real. Yet he also knew somehow that he would return to Orkney. He had fallen in love with these wild islands and warm-hearted people who seemed to thrive in their cold lands.

Alan sipped water while drinking in the company. He

watched fondly as Helen laughed with Shona and Jean, while Callum told stories of difficult seas on the dive boats to David and Laura. It had only been a week since Alan had last eaten there, but it felt like more like a month. Given the laughter and cheer surrounding him, it was hard to believe what had happened.

During a lull in conversation, Jean caught Callum's eye and nodded, to which he spoke up loudly.

'Right… er, I'd, er, just like to say a few things. First off, thanks to Alan for pulling me out m' car and thanks to everyone for helping to sort this mess wi' the plates out. And er, because I have some money left from what Dwight gave me, I'm using it to pay for everyone's meal tonight. Any cash left will go to the RNLI.'

'Wow, that's really generous, Callum,' said Laura, as the rest of the group burst into a round of applause.

Jean nodded at Callum again and tipped her head towards her sister. Callum continued.

'And, er, sorry to Auntie Shona for doubting her. I just hope she can't see any sailors in here tonight!'

After a burst of laughter round the table, Shona looked grave and began speaking.

'Well, actually, I can see a sailor, I'm afraid t' say.' There was silence, until Shona added, 'Aye, Kenny Isbister is in the bar next door wi' my Albie!'

Groans and cackles followed, accompanied by smiles around the table with more than a hint of relief, before the conversations sparked again.

'I heard there was a bit of a to-do at the airport for you, Laura,' said Jean.

Laura flushed a little at the memory, 'Yes, a bit of a shock seeing my ex there.'

'From what Callum said, he won't be bothering you again though,' added Shona.

'Not now I have my own security team,' laughed Laura, smiling at David and Callum.

'Aye, I think David'll keep you safe, right enough. You can always hide out on Hoy with him too!' said Shona.

'That's next week!' smiled Laura. 'He's taking me to the museum for a proper look around and then I'm spending a few days over there.'

'Good for you!' said Shona with a knowing grin as Jean turned to speak to Helen.

'When do you go back to Carlisle?'

'Tomorrow, sadly. But I'll be back in four weeks' time.'

'So soon! There must be a good reason for returning then,' said Shona, grinning again.

'Of course,' said Helen. 'I still haven't seen the Brough of Birsay! And I might catch up with a certain priest too while I'm here. He provides an excellent taxi service, after all!'

Alan turned at the laughing, then tapped the top of his glass with a spoon to create a hush.

'Well, Callum's said a few words, so I thought I'd put my two penneth in as well, as priests are prone to do,' said Alan, to some mock groans. 'I was just thinking how this has been one of the strangest weeks of my life and at times pretty scary. Yet when I look round this table tonight, at the friendship and laughter, I realise these weird events have brought us together. To me, this little group is a blessing out of something horrible that, God willing, is now over. So, I propose a toast – to teamwork and friendship!'

'Teamwork and friendship,' echoed round the table to the clink of glasses.

Then Remi spoke up. 'I'd like to propose a toast too.'

'Another?' said Shona. 'We've had two! We'll be here all bloody night at this rate!'

'Well, I think this is really important,' said Remi, solemnly rising to his feet. 'A toast to the crew of *HMS Vanguard*. May their memory live on and their souls rest in peace.'

EPILOGUE

Laura and David walked hand in hand along Hoy's Rackwick Beach under a soft blue sky, the sea lapping benevolently a few paces to their right. It was a crisp spring morning and they had the whole shoreline to themselves, their footprints making virgin tracks on the golden crescent of sand beyond the thick rim of pebbles.

It had been six months since they'd met in the midst of what they referred to as "the plates issue". Naturally, they thought about it less the more time passed, though as Laura looked out to sea, the sight of a small blue fishing boat with a white wheelhouse acted as a trigger.

'Looks very like the *Peedie Star*,' said Laura.

'Very similar, aye.'

'It's odd, isn't it, thinking back to what happened… y'know, with the plates.'

'I try not to think about it, especially when I'm on my own in the museum. I know Katie's still a bit on edge even though nothing weird's happened since the dive.'

'I think about it less too, but then something'll remind me, like that boat,' said Laura, shuddering briefly as she recalled the way she'd been buffeted, soaked and scared aboard the *Peedie Star* the day Callum had gone overboard.

As if reading her mind, David asked, 'Do y'know how Callum's doing?'

'OK, I think. He's still on the dive boats but has a girlfriend now and another souped-up old Golf to annoy everyone in the village with as he roars up the hill.'

'And you're meeting up with Shona on Friday?'

'Oh yes. The usual Friday drink at Murray's. Oh, and I forgot to tell you, Alan and Helen are joining us.'

'Seems like she's been travelling over here quite a bit,' said David.

'Well, not for much longer.'

'Why not?'

'Because she's retiring and moving here full-time in the summer,' announced Laura.

'Really? What's the bigger pull, Alan or the history?'

'Alan, definitely. I can see them marrying,' said Laura.

'Aye, me too,' said David as they reached the end of the beach and turned to retrace their steps.

'When's Remi coming over?'

'Fourth of July, as befitting an American,' smiled David.

'And his wife and baby are coming too, aren't they?'

'Yeah, he's not just going to be diving this time. He

wants to see something of Orkney with Kim. I said I'd show them round if they wanted because I'm off for the week for the wreck-diving with him anyway.'

'It'll be good to see him again,' said Laura before they walked on in comfortable silence, embracing their surroundings. Suddenly, David stopped and looked intently at the shoreline.

'What's up?' asked Laura.

'I can see something shiny,' said David, stepping quickly towards the water, before bending and pulling an object from the damp sand.

As David turned it over in his hands, brushing the gritty grains from it, Laura could see it was a small, brass cup.

'What is it?' she asked.

'It's a Gill Tot mug and it's stamped 1916 – look!' said David excitedly.

'What's a Gill Tot mug?'

'It's what the Navy used to dole out rum to the sailors. Look, see the ½ Gill on the front. And you can tell it's Royal Navy because of the arrow and GR stamps too! Wow, what a find!'

Once David mentioned it was from a ship, Laura immediately felt uncomfortable.

'I don't like it,' she said flatly.

'What? What don't you like about it? It's a fantastic piece of history! I've never found anything this good on a beach. It's amazing!'

'Well, after what happened with the plates, I just have a bad feeling.'

'But the plates were stolen from a war grave! I've just picked this up! Katie'll love seeing this tomorrow. We could display it in the museum!'

They walked on, trading small talk as David continued glancing at the mug occasionally. Laura's unease grew. She also began to feel as if someone was behind her. Eventually, the feeling compelled her to stop and look round. Her eyes widened at what she saw and when David turned too, his jaw dropped open.

A third set of footprints was pressed into the sand, starting from what appeared to be the spot that David had found the mug. They were a large, heavy tread, clearly made from boots disturbing the sand two paces behind their own prints. Yet no one could be seen.

Laura and David looked at each other and, before anything was said, David threw the mug as far as he could into the sea. Within seconds, the water rushed in far beyond where it had previously reached and splashed around their ankles as they sprinted towards drier sand. When they looked back, the beach had been washed clean.

As they walked briskly back in the direction of the car, nothing was said. They just held on to each other, occasionally looking back, mightily relieved to see only their own footprints behind them as they reached the end of the beach.

HISTORICAL NOTE

While *Souls of Scapa Flow* is a work of fiction, the sinking of *HMS Vanguard* as depicted in the prologue was a real event. I have endeavoured to describe its destruction as accurately as possible from eyewitness accounts of the sinking.

HMS Vanguard was a modern, heavily armed dreadnought battleship over one hundred and sixty metres in length and displacing almost twenty thousand tons. It was built by Vickers at Barrow-in-Furness and commissioned into the Royal Navy in 1910.

HMS Vanguard was assigned to the Home and Grand Fleets and spent its time largely in the North Sea. It was based in Scapa Flow during the war because it offered a protected anchorage, both from the weather and German U-boats. It participated in the largest sea battle of the war at Jutland in May 1916, as expected of one of the Grand Fleet's most powerful vessels.

On the 9th July 1917, *Vanguard* tragically blew up and sank while at anchor in Scapa Flow, close to the island of Hoy. Such was the power of the explosion, a gun turret weighing more than four hundred tons was found on the island of Flotta, having been hurled over a mile from the ship.

Eight hundred and forty-three men on board were killed and there were only two survivors, making the sinking the costliest accidental loss of the twentieth century for the Royal Navy. Only twenty-two bodies were recovered, of which seventeen are buried in Lyness Royal Naval Cemetery on the island of Hoy, where a Celtic cross commemorates the crew.

Given the unexpected nature of the ship's destruction, speculation regarding the cause was rife at the time, including possible sabotage by a spy or German sympathiser. However, the official Court of Inquiry concluded that the probable cause was unstable cordite in one of the gun turrets, which subsequently triggered a sequence of explosions.

Vanguard's wreck lies approximately thirty-four metres down and covers a considerable area, given that the ship was blown apart. The bow and stern are largely intact with a tangled debris field between them. It was subject to salvage operations that removed most of the guns and non-ferrous metals. However, in 1984 it was declared a war grave and in 2002 it was designated as a controlled site. This means it is illegal to dive to the wreck without the permission of the Ministry of Defence.

In 2016, a team of specialist divers surveyed the wreck and produced a detailed report, including photographs that proved extremely useful in helping me to visualise what it would be like to dive to the wreck. It is referenced below and I would recommend looking at the photographs and imaging of the wreck if you are keen to gain an insight into what the wreck is like today.

The following year marked one hundred years since *HMS Vanguard* sank and descendants of the crew laid wreaths above its wreckage. Royal Navy divers also placed a fresh naval ensign on the wreck and a wreath-laying ceremony took place at Lyness Cemetery.

If you are in the fortunate position of being able to travel to Orkney and want to find out more about *HMS Vanguard*, I would recommend visiting Scapa Flow Museum on the island of Hoy and Stromness Museum on the mainland, both of which are featured in the story. Whilst on Hoy, Lyness Royal Naval Military Cemetery is just a short distance by car from the ferry terminal and worth a visit to see the *HMS Vanguard* memorial and the final resting place of some of the crew recovered after the sinking. There are also notable burials from German ships famously scuttled in Scapa Flow in 1919 and from *HMS Royal Oak*, sunk by a German U-boat in 1939 with the loss of eight hundred and thirty-five of its crew. Like *HMS Vanguard*, the *Royal Oak* is a designated war grave and a protected site.

There are three Commonwealth War Graves Commission Naval War Memorials that commemorate the rest of the crew who are not buried at Lyness; six hundred and twenty-one at Chatham, one hundred and twenty-five at Portsmouth and seventy-four at Plymouth.

Many of the dead were teenagers, one of the youngest being Ernest Goddard, who was only fourteen years old. Ernest was a Canteen Assistant Admiralty Civilian and his name can be found on the Portsmouth memorial.

RESEARCH SOURCES

General information regarding *HMS Vanguard*:
https://www.scottishshipwrecks.com/hms-vanguard
Wider historical context and reference to the sinking:
'Scapa' by James Miller (2001). ISBN 1843410052
Wreck survey report:
Turton, E et al (2018). HMS Vanguard 100 Survey 2016 – 2017, Survey Report 2018
Royal Navy coverage of centenary events:
royalnavy.mod.uk/news-and-latest-activity/news/2017/July/07/170707-centenary-of-hmsvanguard-sinking-to-be-marked
BBC coverage of the centenary of the sinking:
bbc.co.uk/news/uk-scotland-north-east-orkney-shetland-40542171
Report of the Court of Enquiry into the sinking:
http://www.gwpda.org/naval/a1373681.htm
Scapa Flow Museum, Hoy, Orkney
Stromness Museum, Orkney

S.D. Read lives in rural North Yorkshire with his wife Carolyn. When he's not stitching words into stories, he enjoys walking his dogs, cycling and visiting places that combine historical interest with natural beauty. Consequently, he is a frequent visitor to Orkney.

ACKNOWLEDGEMENTS

I would like to thank my 'critical friends' Bob Goodrum, Sean Kane, Anne Murphy, Lesley Newton, Ann O'Toole and Lynne Watson, whose encouragement and perceptive observations helped me to develop this story and subsequently seek publication. May I also thank the staff at Scapa Flow Museum who generously provided me with a list of artefacts pertaining to HMS Vanguard currently kept in their display cabinets and, along with Stromness Museum, have allowed me to refer to their excellent museums in the story. I would also like to thank Gina Brown, owner of The Murray Arms in St Margaret's Hope where much of the book is set, for giving permission to refer to her establishment, and for advising me on Orcadian culture and dialect. Last but certainly not least, I am indebted to my wife Carolyn for her unstinting support, advice and forbearance without which *Souls of Scapa Flow* would not have been published.